A Candlelight Ecstasy Romance™

HELPLESS, SHE FELT THE HEAT OF HIS MOUTH MOVING ON HERS. . . .

He was like a warrior home after months of danger and privation. The primitive, compelling demand in his kiss warned against granting him even the smallest kindness. He would swallow it up instantly and demand more. Even now, not satisfied with the taste of her lips, he insisted on the full surrender of her mouth.

Very carefully Reva lifted her hands to his shoulders and tried to push against him, but he hardly seemed to notice.

"Reva, honey," he said hoarsely, his breath warm on her skin. "I could take you here and now. I'm that desperate for you."

CANDLELIGHT ECSTASY ROMANCE™

1 THE TAWNY GOLD MAN, *Amii Lorin*
2 GENTLE PIRATE, *Jayne Castle*
3 THE PASSIONATE TOUCH, *Bonnie Drake*
4 THE SHADOWED REUNION, *Lillian Cheatham*
5 ONLY THE PRESENT, *Noelle Berry McCue*
6 LEAVES OF FIRE, FLAME OF LOVE, *Susan Chatfield*
7 THE GAME IS PLAYED, *Amii Lorin*
8 OCEAN OF REGRETS, *Noelle Berry McCue*
9 SURRENDER BY MOONLIGHT, *Bonnie Drake*
10 GENTLEMAN IN PARADISE, *Harper McBride*
11 MORGAN WADE'S WOMAN, *Amii Lorin*
12 THE TEMPESTUOUS LOVERS, *Suzanne Simmons*
13 THE MARRIAGE SEASON, *Sally Dubois*
14 THE HEART'S AWAKENING, *Valerie Ferris*
15 DESPERATE LONGINGS, *Frances Flores*
16 BESIEGED BY LOVE, *Maryann Young*
17 WAGERED WEEKEND, *Jayne Castle*
18 SWEET EMBER, *Bonnie Drake*
19 TENDER YEARNINGS, *Elaine Raco Chase*
20 THE FACE OF LOVE, *Anne N. Reissner*
21 LOVE'S ENCORE, *Rachel Ryan*

RIGHT
OF
POSSESSION

Jayne Castle

A CANDLELIGHT ECSTASY ROMANCE™

Published by
Dell Publishing Co., Inc.
1 Dag Hammarskjold Plaza
New York, New York 10017

Dell ® TM 681510, Dell Publishing Co., Inc.

Candlelight Ecstasy Romance™ is a trademark of
Dell Publishing Co., Inc., New York, New York.

ISBN: 0-440-17441-4

Printed in the United States of America

First printing—September 1981
Second printing—September 1981

Dear Reader:

In response to your enthusiasm for Candlelight Ectasy Romances™, we are now increasing the number of titles per month from two to three.

We are pleased to offer you sensuous novels set in America, depicting modern American women and men as they confront the provocative problems of a modern relationship.

Throughout the history of the Candlelight line, Dell has tried to maintain a high standard of excellence, to give you the finest in reading pleasure. It is now and will remain our most ardent ambition.

Vivian Stephens
Editor
Candlelight Romances

CHAPTER ONE

Reva Waring, halfway through an excellent veal à la Marsala, was pausing to take a sip of the '74 Chardonnay her escort had selected when something made her glance idly toward the restaurant entrance. Her shock at the sight of the tall, broad-shouldered man filling the doorway nearly caused her to drop the long-stemmed glass.

"Something wrong?" Bruce Tanner's polite inquiry brought Reva's elegantly neat head around and she carefully smiled her coolly charming smile. Reva was very good at recovering her poise in an instant. It was a skill developed on the road up through management in the business world. At twenty-nine Reva felt there was little that could crack her self-possession, but the sight of the man in the doorway had done it for a few incredible seconds. She had convinced herself during the past four months that he would never really make good on his promise. She should have known better.

"I thought I saw someone I recognized," she said smoothly to the attractive blond-haired, blue-eyed man sitting across the table. And, she added silently to herself, I can only hope he didn't recognize me. But that was a futile wish, she thought with grim honesty. The sole explanation for Josh Corbett's presence in this particular Portland, Oregon, restaurant was that he had come for her.

7

Exactly as he had told her he would four months ago. That had been at dawn on a desolate airfield in a tiny South American nation the name of which Reva had consciously tried to forget. And the tall, tough man with the dark-brown hair and the lion-colored eyes hadn't asked if she wanted him to come for her. He'd simply said, "Wait for me. I'll come for you as soon as this is over."

Then he'd helped Reva into the old DC-3, handed the expatriot, gunrunning American pilot a large amount of U.S. currency, and walked away into the rising morning heat of yet another Latin American country torn apart by revolution. Reva had sat in the copilot's seat, the plane's only passenger, and watched, with an unwarranted sense of loss, Josh Corbett disappear from her life. It was only later that the relief began to set in.

"A business associate?" Bruce Tanner asked quickly. Bruce understood the importance of business associates. "If you catch his eye, feel free to invite him to join us for a drink later." He flicked back the silk cuff at his wrist and scanned the sophisticated, amazingly thin gold watch he was wearing. "We should be through here in another twenty minutes. I'll be quite happy to meet him." His handsome features conveyed his perfect understanding of the situation.

One thing about Bruce, Reva thought fleetingly, he could be fully counted upon to encourage a woman in her career. He would never dream of asking her to sacrifice everything for him. Not as Hugh Tyson had done four years ago. But then, Reva reminded herself, she would never be so foolish as to agree to the sacrifice as she had agreed to Hugh's request when she was twenty-five. She'd learned her lesson!

"That won't be necessary. If it was who I thought it was, he's not someone from the office. Just a man I met several months back," Reva explained quietly, bending her head to concentrate her blue-green eyes on the veal. The sea-colored eyes looked out on the world from behind a pair of chic designer frames and it occurred to Reva that Josh might be scanning the subtly lit restaurant for women wearing glasses. She seriously considered removing them but decided that would only elicit more questions from Bruce. Perhaps if she kept her head down, she thought a little desperately, the glasses wouldn't be so visible. With luck the searching man wouldn't recognize her hair. During the three days Josh had known her the sun-washed brown stuff had been a straggling, unkempt mess. Tonight the heavy shoulder-length tresses were gathered into a sleek, graceful knot at the nape of her neck.

"Oh, well," Bruce was saying casually, losing interest in the unknown male, "if he's not someone important . . ."

"No, he's no one important," Reva assured him. At least, she went on mentally, he's no longer important. Only for those horrible days in that damn little country had he been important. But she had deliberately tried to forget that aberration in her life and Josh Corbett along with it. She had never seriously thought he'd come looking for her. Or had she? Was that the real reason she'd taken it into her head to quietly change apartments shortly after returning from the abortive vacation to South America? She had told herself and her friends she was moving to get a better view of the Willamette River, but had she subconsciously felt a little safer changing addresses?

Now what was she going to do, Reva asked herself grimly. There was only one rational answer, of course. She would be coolly polite if Josh spotted her in the crowd and approached the table. Yes, cool and gracious and formal. That would be the ticket. If he was at all perceptive he

9

would get the hint immediately. And she had Bruce with her, didn't she? Surely that would provide a neat barrier.

"How's the veal?" the neat barrier interrupted her chasing thoughts to ask. "This scampi is excellent. And the Chardonnay isn't bad, although it seemed to me the wine list was a bit limited." A serious, considering expression knit Bruce's handsome brow as he waited for Reva's comments.

She risked a glance upward to meet his intent blue eyes and smiled once again. The large man she had seen in the doorway was no longer in her field of vision. Perhaps he'd left. The hopeful thought helped relax Reva's somewhat taut features. She was not a beautiful woman but the firm line of a feminine chin, the regal nose, and high cheekbones came together in an intelligent, almost striking profile. Reva had long ago learned to capitalize on that, using the bold frames of her glasses, the smooth, businesslike style of her hair and perfectly tailored clothes, to pull together an image that radiated ability, confidence, and success. If she could have taken part in the design of her own body she would have given herself more height to go with her small-boned figure. Either that, she'd decided, or less of an appreciation for good food. As it was, nearly constant dieting was necessary to keep her five-foot-five-inch frame pared to the fashionably sleek silhouette she preferred. Of course, she could have eaten better at home during the week if she didn't allow herself to splurge on the weekends with meals such as the one she was enjoying tonight. Or had been enjoying, she corrected.

"The meal is quite perfect, Bruce, as I'm sure you know. You have a knack for picking the best places. I've thoroughly enjoyed all of our evenings out this past month." And it was the truth, Reva thought with a sense of satisfaction marred only by her inner fear that Josh

10

Corbett hadn't really left the restaurant. Bruce Tanner was beginning to look like the perfect mate for her. Now, at twenty-nine, with her career firmly reestablished after the disastrous mistake she'd made at twenty-five, Reva had decided it was time to marry. Bruce was one year older and offered everything she needed in a man.

"Thanks, Reva," he began with a pleased smile. "I want you to know this past month has been very good for me, too. We seem quite suited, you and I. We're both career-oriented, we both enjoy the same things, and . . ." He broke off to glance upward in surprise at the stranger who had come to a halt by Reva's shoulder.

But Reva hadn't needed to see the politely inquiring expression on her escort's face. She had sensed the large, quiet presence an instant earlier and was already composing herself for the next few minutes. She could handle this, she told herself resolutely. She was back on her own territory and here there would be no problem dealing with Josh Corbett.

"Hello, Reva," he said in that deep, dark, faintly southwestern drawl which brought back those three days in South America as if they had only ended yesterday. "Still having nightmares?"

Reva felt herself whiten at the words. In spite of all her brave knowledge of her own ability to handle unpleasant situations, she couldn't keep the blood from seeping momentarily from her face and then rushing fiercely back. How could he, after four months, have asked the one question which was perfectly calculated to remind her of that last night? It had been deliberate on his part and Reva knew of no other man who, after a long absence, would walk up to a woman in a public restaurant and issue a point-blank challenge to recall her surrender in his arms.

With all her not inconsiderable will, Reva determined that this man should not see her reaction.

"Hello, Josh," she smiled with a semblance of polite surprise and pleasure. She lifted her eyes to meet the lion-colored gaze and collided with the totally undisguised intent she saw there. "How nice to see you again. It's been a long time."

She allowed herself to study the weathered, granite-hard face with the socially acceptable curiosity of casual acquaintances who chance to run into one another. Josh Corbett was thirty-eight years old and every line on his craggy face indicated that those years had not been spent pursuing the gentler side of life. His skin was deeply, probably permanently tanned. Fine lines radiated from the corners of the honey-brown eyes which reminded her so much of a lion's gaze and deeper grooves marked the edges of his hard mouth. An aggressive blade of a nose and tightly drawn, commanding cheekbones paired with the heavy dark brows and strong chin to give the man an utterly uncompromising look. The gray she had remembered flecking his temples was still there in the deep-brown hair, a bit more noticeable now that he'd had a recent haircut. And Josh Corbett had the slightly more than six feet of height to carry off the overall impression of tough, hard-bitten male. Large, lean, and potentially lethal. Then Reva's carefully remote glance fell on the tie.

In spite of her resolve, she blinked in astonishment. Never in a million years would she have imagined this man choosing to wear the brilliant, crimson-striped thing. The conventional dark suit, white shirt, and polished shoes, yes. They somehow added to the quiet look of subtle male menace. But the gorgeous tie was wildly out of character, she thought wryly. Or was it? There was something about it which said its owner would only go so far to satisfy the dictates of society. Beyond a certain point Josh Corbett didn't give a damn what others thought. Reva wrenched her gaze quickly away from the fascinating tie as Josh responded to her greeting.

"It's been exactly four months," he noted, his gaze locking with hers. "What's the matter, Reva, didn't you think I'd remember to come and collect you when I had finished my business in South America?"

Reva swallowed, knowing he was asking her why she was out with Bruce Tanner when she was supposed to be at home, patiently waiting to be "collected." She quelled the stirring of resentful anger which threatened to make her say something rude. She owed this man a lot. The bare truth was that he had saved her life. But that had never given him the right to assume she had any intention of going back to the real world and waiting for him! She certainly had made no commitments on that scale, in spite of what he may have concluded that last night. . . .

"Bruce, I'd like you to meet Josh Corbett. He and I met several months ago while I was vacationing. Josh, this is Bruce Tanner, a very close friend." She let the last three words fall with the smallest of meaningful stresses.

"Pleased to meet you, Corbett," Bruce said pleasantly, politely averting his eyes from the crimson tie and extending his hand in a genial masculine gesture. He smiled at the older man who only topped him by about three inches but who seemed to dwarf him, nevertheless. Next to Josh, Bruce looked soft and very, very civilized.

"How do you do, Mr. Tanner," Josh said with gravelly politeness, accepting the proffered hand and shaking it once. Once was enough, Reva knew, as her escort hurriedly withdrew his white-knuckled fingers. She gritted her teeth. The small display of muscle had been entirely unnecessary and incredibly impolite. Exactly what one could

13

expect from a man like Corbett. Before she could say anything to bring the small scene to a decently swift conclusion, however, Josh was continuing to speak to Bruce.

"If you'll excuse me," he went on in a deceptively bland voice, "I'll take Reva home now." He put out a hand and closed steel fingers around one of her slender wrists.

"Josh!" Reva stared at him, furious and still faintly disbelieving. She was painfully aware of Bruce's uncomfortable confusion. "Don't be ridiculous," she said sternly, not rising in response to the gentle tug on her hand. "I'm here with Bruce tonight. It's nice to see you again and I certainly hope you'll enjoy your stay here in Portland, but I have no intention of accompanying you anywhere. Especially not tonight when, as you can see, I have other plans." She lifted her chin and narrowed her blue-green eyes at him through the lenses of her glasses. The man belonged in that jungle where she had left him! "You can call me in the morning. . . ."

Josh turned his attention back to her, the lion eyes resting searchingly on her tense, forbidding expression. And then the corner of his mouth quirked upward in a small flash of genuine humor combined with admonishment.

"You really didn't think I'd come for you, did you?" he murmured chidingly. "But I'm here, Reva, and everything's going to be fine."

He made no further move to force her to her feet, but neither did he release her wrist, and Reva had the horrifying notion that he was capable of simply picking her up and walking out of the restaurant if she proved too uncooperative. She had to get a handle on the situation immediately or risk a major scene. Bruce would never forgive that.

"Please, Josh," she smiled with careful wry humor,

"you're certainly not going to embarrass me, are you? Why don't you sit down and have a glass of wine with us while we finish eating and you can tell me what you've been doing lately."

"Yes, do join us for a few minutes, Corbett," Bruce put in coolly, his eyes flicking first to Reva and then to the man standing solidly beside her. Reva could almost feel him deciding to follow her lead in dealing with the unexpected difficulty the stranger represented. She quashed the disloyal thought that wished her date for the evening were a bit more aggressive in handling the matter. "There's some of the Chardonnay left," Bruce added, indicating the wine bucket positioned at the side of the table. "I'm sure we can get the waiter to bring another glass."

"Thank you," Josh returned with soft mockery. "But it's been four months since I last saw Reva and I have a great deal to say to her. In private." He glanced down into Reva's angrily upturned face. "Come along, honey. If you're still hungry we'll pick something up on the way home. I'm quite capable of keeping you fed, if you remember."

Reva, whose normally healthy appetite had totally deserted her, frowned furiously up into Josh's hard expectant face. His eyes met hers in casual promise and she knew with clear resignation that he had no qualms at all about making a scene if that's what it would take to make her leave with him. Perhaps the best solution was to do exactly that and get the inevitable confrontation over. It was undoubtedly going to take some doing convincing him that she certainly had no intention of picking up where she'd left off four months ago. Those three days were a totally abnormal time in her life and she did not honestly feel she could be held responsible for her behavior. She would have to make Josh Corbett understand

15

that. She turned apologetically to Bruce, who plainly found the situation incomprehensible.

"I'm sorry, Bruce, but I'm afraid this is going to be a little awkward. Mr. Corbett seems to think our short acquaintance of four months ago entitles him to impose on me now." She didn't look at Josh as she said the deliberately rude words but she felt the fingers on her wrist tighten ever so slightly. Well, what did he expect? Why should she be any kinder to him than he was being to her by embarrassing her in front of Bruce?

"There's no need for you to leave if you'd rather not, Reva," Bruce said with unexpected authority.

She smiled at him, a genuinely appreciative smile that conveyed her thanks. "I know, Bruce, but I think it would be better if I handled the matter quietly. Mr. Corbett will soon be on his way, believe me. Forgive me for cutting the evening short. It was most delightful while it lasted. . . ." She let the sentence trail off delicately, the full implication of how Josh Corbett was ruining the evening settling nicely.

"Vicious little thing, isn't she?" Josh observed mildly, one dark brow lifting in acknowledgment of the cut.

"Miss Waring is never vicious!" Bruce informed him coldly.

"Except when she's provoked, and when the provocation is sufficient you'd better hope you're not facing her when she's got a knife in her hand!"

"Josh Corbett!" Reva flared, unable to completely repress the mental image he was forcing alive in her head. With it came remembered terror, fury, and desperation. For a ghastly instant she was again facing a young revolutionary guerrilla, his dark eyes wild with war lust. The carving knife she'd found in an abandoned kitchen had been her only defense. But in the end she'd not had to use it. Josh Corbett had appeared out of nowhere, a rifle slung over one shoulder and an automatic in his hand. It had been the automatic which had spoken. . . . Grimly she forced herself back to the present.

"Let's go, Reva," Josh said calmly, "I've been waiting too long already." He tugged once again at her wrist.

"I'll summon the manager," Bruce announced with great decisiveness. He flung down his napkin and got to his feet, glaring at the taller man.

"No, Bruce, I can handle this," Reva interposed quickly, rising to her feet also in response to the light pressure Josh was applying. The important thing was to prevent a scene which would humiliate Bruce and herself. And that meant leaving with Josh. "Mr. Corbett means no harm," she sighed, her eyes on Bruce's incensed features. "He's just not accustomed to the ways of normal, civilized society," she added meaningfully. "I'd better have a long talk with him and it would be less uncomfortable for all of us if I did it in private. Forgive me?" she smiled with rueful appeal as Josh made to move off with herself in tow. He was no longer interested in Bruce, who was obviously not going to make any move to stop him.

"I'll phone you in the morning," Bruce stated emphatically. "You're sure you'll be all right?" Clearly he wanted a way out of the situation, too.

"Quite all right." She grabbed her gold evening bag and the shawl which matched her long silk sheath.

"Very well, but I don't care for your attitude one bit, Corbett!" Bruce informed the other man disdainfully.

"I wasn't overly pleased to find you out with Reva, either." Josh smiled with a very feral expression. "But we must be gentlemen about this, mustn't we?" he added sardonically, starting down the row of interested diners seated nearby.

17

With a last, reassuring glance at Bruce, Reva stopped trying to resist the chain on her wrist and allowed herself to be led past the astonished maitre d' and out into the chill night air of the late Oregon fall. It took all her willpower to keep from screaming at her captor. Only the years of practice in dealing with the various temperaments of corporate management enabled Reva to maintain some outward appearance of cool hauteur. She might owe this man her life, but she would never forgive him for coming back into it.

"All right, Josh," she stated evenly as the door to the restaurant swung shut behind them. "You've had your big scene. There's no need to continue dragging me along like this. I've agreed to come peacefully."

But he wasn't listening to her. Instead, he'd halted beside a long black car parked illegally at the curb and was fishing out a set of keys. With an economy of movement that brought back memories to Reva, he handed her into the front seat, slammed the door, and went rapidly around to the driver's side.

An instant later he was sliding in beside her, reaching for her with his large competent hands, his face drawn and intent. Instinctively Reva tried to edge away. In the confines of the car he seemed large and overpowering. But he appeared unaware of her attempt at retreat, clamping his fingers around her shoulders and holding her still in front of him as he sat twisted in the driver's seat. The lion eyes raked her as if, in the relative privacy of the car, they could finally drink their fill.

"Reva, Reva, honey," he growled in a husky whisper. "It's been four long months. God! How I've ached for you, woman! Do you know that?" He shook his dark head in rueful relief and the fingers on her shoulders clenched and unclenched with a strange urgency.

In the dim light of the street lamps Reva noticed the small things she hadn't had time to become aware of in the restaurant. He was just as hard and lean as she had remembered but the silver at his temples lent a surprisingly distinguished look which hadn't been so noticeable four months ago when his hair had been longer and he'd had a couple days' growth of rough beard. The expensive material of his dark suit and crisp white shirt was a definite improvement over the khaki slacks and shirt she'd last seen him wearing, Reva decided. He looked, in fact, quite presentable if one ignored the crimson slash of his tie, she told herself wryly. But he didn't fool her for a moment.

"I'm glad you're out of that mess safe and sound," Reva said politely, her body stiff and resisting in his grasp. The shawl she'd wrapped around the shoulders of the long-sleeved, iridescent silk dress provided some protection from the strength of his fingers, but not much. She could feel them biting gently into her flesh.

"Were you worried about me?" he asked softly, and she had the impression he would have been pleased with her concern. He released her shoulders abruptly to cup her face between roughly gentle hands.

"Frankly, no." Reva shrugged with deliberate callousness. Never would she let him know how many nights she'd awakened from the nightmares and stared at the ceiling, wondering what had become of him. She rarely had those dreams anymore. It had been only during that first month that she'd dreaded going to sleep. "You seemed to know what you were doing." Josh Corbett didn't need anyone to worry about him!

"I'll assume that's some kind of compliment," he said flatly, watching her cool eyes with a kind of hunger. "Although I wondered at first if that wasn't the reason you were out with that boy tonight. . . ."

"If what wasn't the reason?" Reva demanded.

"If you'd convinced yourself I hadn't made it back to the States I could see why you might have tried to console yourself with someone else," he explained patiently.

"Josh, let's get something very clear between us," Reva said carefully, determinedly. "I was out with Bruce tonight because I wanted to go out with him. I am, in fact, considering marriage to him. I have not spent the last four months pining for you. I was very grateful to you, of course, but I don't recall ever giving you the impression that I expected you to look me up when you got back!"

"But I'm here, Reva," he said calmly, "and I don't believe you. You must have been expecting me because I told you to expect me." Such vast, complete assurance, Reva thought a little dizzily. How did one combat it?

"Josh, what happened between us was over four months ago when you put me on that plane. You know that as well as I do. We had nothing holding us together except the business of trying to stay alive. I admit I could never have made it without you," Reva said with passionate honesty, "but you can't have mistaken my gratitude for some undying love. During those three days I told you something of my life and my career. Surely you understood that our backgrounds were completely different, completely incompatible. . . ."

"You didn't answer my question in the restaurant," he interrupted gently. "Do you still have the nightmare?"

"No," she lied heavily, "and it would be none of your business if I did!"

The honey of his eyes flowed over her face, soft and hungry, and Reva knew he hadn't listened to a thing she had said.

"I'll take you home, Reva," he said deeply. "We have a lot of lost time to make up. But first . . ." He broke off his words abruptly and bent his head as if he could no longer resist the temptation of her mouth. Holding her face carefully and firmly, Josh took her lips in a sudden, fiercely possessive kiss filled with barely restrained raw male hunger.

Helpless, Reva felt the heat of his mouth moving on hers, tasting, exploring, relearning. He was like a warrior home after months of danger and privation. Such men went a little crazy at first. Everyone knew that, Reva assured herself. And if a man has convinced himself that there is a certain woman waiting for him it made sense he might seek her out, expecting a warm welcome. Shouldn't she be a little patient with this man who had saved her life?

But the primitive, compelling demand in his kiss warned against granting him even the smallest of kindnesses. He would only swallow them up and instantly demand more even, as now, when he was unsatisfied with the taste of her lips, he began insisting on the full surrender of her mouth.

Very carefully Reva lifted her hands to his shoulders and tried to push against him, but he hardly seemed to notice.

"Reva, honey," he grated at the corner of her mouth, his breath warm on her skin, "I could take you here and now in the back seat of this damn car, I'm that desperate for you!"

His hands still cupping her face, Josh moved his thumbs to the edge of her lips, forcing them apart. Reva tried to protest but the small sound was drowned beneath his heavier groan of passion as his tongue swept into the undefended valley of her mouth, plundering the warmth it found there.

A tiny, numbing edge of panic began to filter through Reva's awareness. Things were getting out of hand. His weight shifted unexpectedly as he lowered strong fingers to her waist to pull her more tightly against him. Reva took the opportunity to struggle in earnest, turning her head to the side. The small action jarred her glasses, knocking them askew, and she instantly reached up to rescue them.

The little gesture was enough to cause Josh reluctantly to lift his head, his gold cat eyes flaming softly down at her as she made a production out of straightening the chic frames and righting her shawl. She didn't look at him.

"Sorry, honey," he apologized with a wry grin, running the hand at her waist up and down her spine as he watched her put herself to rights. "A car is definitely not the place to show you how much I've missed you. But you do look kind of cute with those funny glasses tilted on your nose and your hair starting to come apart."

Reva hastily tucked in the strands of light-brown hair which had loosened from the neat bundle at her nape. Funny glasses, indeed! Those frames had cost almost a hundred dollars. She didn't know why that particular remark bothered her, but it did.

"If you're quite through with the welcome demonstration, would you mind taking me on home?" she said with chilling politeness, sliding as far as possible into her corner of the seat and fastening the lap belt.

"Home is exactly where I want to take you," he replied in a low, velvety voice that made her glance up warily. His eyes never left her taut profile.

"You don't seem to have heard a word I've said this evening, Josh," she sighed. "Please don't play stupid. We both know you're not. I'm trying very hard to be patient and polite but you must see that I'm not going to pretend that I came back from that jungle with any notion of perpetuating our . . . our relationship! As I said earlier, I'm glad you're safely back, but you can't really expect me to throw myself into your arms." She swung around to frown appealingly at him in the shadows. "Josh, those three days were a nightmare I've put behind me. I just want to forget the whole thing. I've come back to my safe and sane life here in the city and everything is back on track. I just want to forget it! Can't you understand that?"

"You can forget the bad part, honey," Josh said gently, his arm resting lightly on the steering wheel as he studied her. "But you can't forget me. I won't let you," he added simply. He turned and flicked on the engine. "I agree that we should go home, though—this car is cold and I feel the overpowering need for more privacy than it can provide!"

Reva drew a slow, steadying breath. She could deal with this. She could deal with almost anything. Patience, firmness, and determination were called for here. She said nothing as Josh guided the car away from the curb and out into traffic. Nor did she volunteer any directions. He had clearly found her address once already this evening. That thought did bring on a question, however.

"How did you know I was at the restaurant?" she asked distantly, her gaze on the city lights.

"Your next-door neighbor told me. She heard me knocking and looked out to see who was there in the hallway." Josh slanted his passenger an enigmatic look. "I explained who I was and she told me you'd gone out."

"How, exactly, did you explain yourself to Sandy?" Reva asked with great foreboding.

"I told her the truth, of course," he returned with a dismissing shrug. "I explained I'd come to find you and marry you."

"Marry me!" Reva was stunned at his audacity. "You told Sandy you'd come to marry me? My God! She must still be howling with laughter. Oh, Josh, how could you

23

do such a thing? Even you must have some notion of behavior. You can't have lived your whole life in that horrid little country!" Reva collapsed in disgust, sinking deeply into the seat.

"But I am going to marry you, honey," he informed her quietly, and then he slanted her a softened glance. "Did you think I wasn't intending something permanent? Is that why you were so upset this evening when you realized I'd arrived? You thought I'd only come back for a brief affair?"

"No," she retorted grimly. "That was not my main concern! Whatever affair we were fated to have is well and truly over!"

"I remember three days of keeping you safe," he mused, "and two nights of keeping you warm while you slept, utterly exhausted, curled against me like a kitten. And I remember the third night when you awoke with nightmares. . . ."

"Please, Josh," she begged, his words reviving sternly suppressed images.

"And when I comforted you," he continued ruthlessly, "you turned to me like a flower to the sun. I'd never wanted a woman as much as I wanted you that night, Reva, and when we made love I could tell the feeling was mutual. You were all soft passion and fire and . . ."

"Stop it!" Reva snarled, turning her head to glare furiously at him. "I was a frightened, overwrought, and exceedingly grateful woman. You represented the only safety and security to be had in that hell. It was only natural I let you make love to me. It was . . . it was a kind of *instinct!*" With bitter resolve Reva used on him the same arguments and explanations she'd given herself for weeks after returning to the States. She had been caught up in a dangerous, primitive situation with a man who had

24

risked his life for her. It was only natural that she had responded to him when he'd made love to her in the darkness of that abandoned hut on the edge of the jungle.

"I'll go along with that," Josh grated deeply, turning toward the waterfront. "It was instinct. An instinct freed by the trauma of the situation and which can be freed again. Just because you've spent four months trying to pretend it didn't happen doesn't mean you won't still feel the same things tonight when I hold you again, Reva, honey."

Reva took a determined grip on her temper. "You're not going to spend the night with me, Josh. There's no going back to that night four months ago. It was a fluke, a once-in-a-lifetime situation which will never again be repeated. You and I are as opposite as it's possible for two human beings to be. Marriage between us or even an affair is something I can't possibly consider. You must understand that. You can take me home tonight and I'll even give you a cup of coffee or a nightcap, God knows I owe you that much, I suppose. But after that you'll leave. You'll *have* to leave. I have my own life to live and it would never in a million years be compatible with yours."

"What makes you so sure of that?" he asked with a half smile as he unerringly located the high-rise apartment building Reva called home and found a parking space on the street in front. He didn't seem overly concerned about the forcefulness of her arguments, merely curious, Reva thought in annoyance.

"I'm not a teen-ager, Josh. I'm aware of what it takes to make a good, lasting relationship. And it involves far more than lust! You . . . you obviously have a much different background from mine. You're at home carrying a rifle in a jungle. You can commit an act of violence and not wake up three nights later having nightmares. I was in the middle of that mess in South America because I was an innocent tourist caught in the wrong place at the wrong time. But that's not why you were there, is it, Josh?" she challenged.

"No," he agreed quietly, opening his door. "It's not why I was there." He closed the door firmly on any further comments she would have made on the subject. When he appeared on the other side of the car to help her out onto the street, he merely said, "We'll talk about that some other time. Come along and give me that nightcap you promised."

"You give me your word you won't be difficult when I ask you to leave?" she demanded as he walked her toward the entrance.

"I wouldn't think of being 'difficult,' " he told her dryly. "I've come home to marry you, little one, what's so difficult about that?" He folded an arm around her waist as they walked, anchoring her close to his side.

"Josh," Reva declared flatly, "I'm not going to let you come up to my apartment if you're going to . . . to assault me!"

"Assault you!" He looked thunderstruck at the accusation, coming to a halt on the sidewalk and swinging her around to face him. "Look at me, Reva Waring! Do you really believe that after all we've shared together I'd ever hurt you? That I'd ever *assault* you?"

Reva, slightly astonished by his unexpected resentment of the warning, blinked uncertainly up into his stern features, saw the narrowed signs of offense in the lion eyes, and relented.

"I . . . I didn't mean to imply," she began hesitantly, "that you would . . ."

"Rape you?" he concluded baldly, his anger very visible.

26

"Yes."

For a long moment he held her eyes and then, with a faint inclination of his dark head which acknowledged her poor apology, he turned to continue the walk to the apartment building.

"I would have been on your doorstep a few days ago," he told her as they entered the lobby. "Why in hell didn't you leave a forwarding address with the manager of your last apartment building? Did you really not believe I'd come for you?" He shook his head as if he simply couldn't comprehend her lack of faith in his promise.

Reva didn't look at him as she punched the elevator button. How could she say that the reason she'd left no address at the last place was because some small part of her had feared he *would* come?

"I've torn this town apart for four days looking for you, do you realize that?" Josh went on in an almost neutral tone as they stepped into the elevator. He reached out and lifted her chin between thumb and forefinger so that she had to meet his gaze. He was smiling with a strange kind of wonder. "But that's all over," he declared roughly. "I can forget all the little problems now that I've found you. I sure haven't slept worth a damn for the past few nights, though, knowing you were somewhere in the city and not being able to put my hands on you."

"How did you find my new address?" Reva asked in resignation. She should have guessed that just moving wouldn't slow him down much.

"I remembered your telling me that you work for a large manufacturing firm but you hadn't mentioned the name. I've spent a lot of time on the telephone during the past few days," he admitted as the elevator came to a halt. "When I finally did locate the right company there was some, uh, reluctance to give out your home address."

Reva glanced at him sharply. "How did you get Personnel to divulge it?"

"A little pressure applied in the right places can work miracles," he assured her, taking the key out of her hand and fitting it into the door.

"Oh, Josh," she groaned as he pushed her gently before him into the apartment. "I have a business reputation to protect. I hope you didn't do anything . . ."

Her words were cut off as a dark-gray shape, poised in front of the window overlooking the city, moved with a soft growl and padded toward her. Reva flicked on a light and half-smiled as the huge, battle-scarred alley cat came forward to investigate the stranger she had brought home.

"I see you've been well looked after while I was gone," Josh said, hunkering down to stare into the eyes of the big cat, who returned the gaze with interest. For a long moment the two regarded each other silently and it occurred to Reva they probably had a lot in common. Then the cat touched his nose to the tip of Josh's hand, flicked his tail in satisfaction, and walked silently back to his window seat. Josh stood and turned to look inquiringly at Reva.

"That's Xavier," she explained, slipping off her shawl. "He adopted me shortly before I moved here. I told him he wasn't going to like living in a high-rise building, but he doesn't seem to mind."

"Because he's decided home is where you are," Josh murmured, helping her with the shawl. "Cats are highly adaptable. It's a survival characteristic, you see. I understand Xavier's decision completely." Reva saw the warning in his eyes too late.

An instant later she was hauled into his overwhelming embrace, crushed against the material of his jacket as he

28

wrapped her close against his hard leanness.

"Reva, honey, I've been waiting four months for this moment," he rasped in her ear. "Tomorrow will be time enough to talk out the details. Tonight I must have you in my bed!"

CHAPTER TWO

Reva only barely managed to wedge her hands against his broad chest as Josh once again sought her mouth with his own.

"Josh!" she gasped angrily. "You promised!"

"This won't be rape, little one," he soothed, his lips lazing hungrily over the skin of her cheek as she turned her head to the side. "We're going to make love, you and I."

"No! Stop it this minute, Josh Corbett, you've already had a welcome-home kiss and that's all you're going to get!" Reva stormed. She wasn't really frightened, not yet. But she was vastly annoyed, and her blue-green eyes darkened behind her glasses as she tried to struggle without creating so much racket her next-door neighbors would be drawn to the scene.

"That wasn't a welcome-home kiss back there in the car," Josh scolded lightly, his large hands tightening gently but with incredible strength. "That was just a little something I grabbed on the run until I could get the full meal. Don't you know me well enough after those three days to remember that all my appetites are large? I distinctly recall that, once aroused, none of yours were particularly small, either!"

"Josh! What an awful thing to say!" Reva declared

furiously. She grew impatient with his deepening embrace and deliberately dug her fingers into the vulnerable area at the base of his neck. "Now let me go or I'll . . . No!" The last word came out in a small, horrified yelp as he suddenly bent and lifted her high into his arms. It had the immediate effect of causing her to stop the small punishment she had begun with her hands. Instead she instinctively splayed her fingers, clutching to keep from falling.

"That's better," he approved huskily as he felt her automatically cling, and then he was striding across the off-white carpet to sit down heavily on the Chinese red sofa. Reva found herself sprawled across his lap and before she could regain her equilibrium his mouth had at last closed over hers.

Her initial annoyance and dismay at having discovered Josh Corbett was a man of his word had protected her in the car outside the restaurant. She had felt the desire in him then as if it were a leashed panther and had been appalled, wanting only to step back out of reach. But now he was holding her, cradling her the way he had cradled her against him that last night in the jungle, and the heat of his body reached out to enfold her as it had then. Memories of her response on that occasion sprang far too vividly to life. Memories she wanted very badly to forget.

"Reva, my sweet Reva," Josh growled, his voice dark and heavy with undisguised desire. "You can't have forgotten what we had four months ago."

"It was such a short time, Josh," she protested weakly, striving desperately to summon her common sense. "We hardly knew each other then and . . . and we know each other even less now!"

"That's not true," he retorted coaxingly, holding her with one hand and stroking her curving body with the other. His mouth nuzzled the soft, sensitive area behind her ear. "We hid nothing from each other during those three days. And it's only you who are trying to hide things now. But I know too much about you to believe the cool, remote little facade you were attempting to erect between us in the restaurant. That might work with boys like Tanner, but not with me." His hand stopped moving back and forth from her shoulder to her thigh and instead paused to lift the glasses away from her face, setting them down cautiously on the polished lacquer table nearby.

"I thought it was women who were supposed to be guilty of . . . of romanticizing brief encounters," Reva tried to say mockingly, holding herself stiffly but no longer actively fighting him. Something told her that physical resistance at this stage would simply be ignored by Josh. It wasn't that he was the sort of man to enjoy forcibly overcoming a woman, he just wouldn't find her attempt at battle very important. Not when he was so certain in his own mind that they both wanted each other.

"Romanticizing! Is that what you think I'm doing, woman?" He abruptly laughed, a deep sound from far down in his chest. "Let me tell you exactly how I remember those three days and you tell me if you honestly think I'm guilty of romanticizing them. First off, I distinctly recall that the only bath either of us had during the whole time was one quick dip in a river on the second day. I also vividly remember you complaining about being hungry most of the time. . . ."

"I did not!" Reva felt obliged to defend herself against the accusation. Her neat brows drew together in a quelling frown.

"Yes, you did. So much so that in order to pacify you I was forced to stoop to 'liberating' a few chickens, several eggs, and bartering my watch for some milk!" The lion gaze gleamed humorously down into her upturned face.

33

"You were just as hungry as I was!" she shot back tartly. But against her will she was remembering that he had kept her fed during those three days. Even if she'd been able to catch the chickens by herself she wasn't at all sure she could have killed and cleaned them. Her only contribution to their meals had been cooking and serving. It was Josh who had calmly disappeared in the brief hours before dawn and returned with food from sources he refused to specify.

"Oh, I was hungry, all right," he agreed, toying with a lock of sun-streaked hair which had fallen across her shoulder. Then his eyes swept the slender shape of her body, taking in the small breasts and narrow waist outlined beneath the glimmering silk sheath. "But you don't look as if you've been eating as well lately as you were when I was responsible for feeding you," he noted. "Hell, woman! I can feel your bones!" He ran probing fingers lightly over the shape of her hip and frowned. "Are you sure you haven't been pining away for me?" he added.

"Not in the least. I've been dieting. The only reason I had more weight on me when you saw me last is that I'd been vacationing for several days and I always go on a binge during vacations!" Reva fixed him with a look of hauteur.

"You didn't look as if you were dieting tonight," he remarked.

"When I eat out I enjoy myself. But I have to make up for it by watching calories the rest of the week," she sighed, wondering how in the world the subject of the conversation had become her eating habits.

"Trying to stay fashionably skinny for boys like Tanner? Well, you won't have to worry about that around me. I already know you have a healthy appetite and I wouldn't mind in the least if you increase by a couple of sizes. I doubt that it's even healthy being this slender."

"Josh! Will you kindly talk about something else? My diet problems are my own affair!" Reva snapped. Very delicately she attempted to straighten slightly in his lap but without a word he simply tightened his hold and she was forced tenderly back against him.

"What was the original subject?" he mused thoughtfully. "Oh, yes, your concern that I may have overromanticized our encounter four months ago. Let's see, what else do I remember?"

"Okay," she groaned in resignation, "So you recall some of the difficulties involved. But you're missing my whole point, Josh, and that is that you seem to have developed some sort of fixation about me which probably came about because of the drama of the moment. You stayed behind and I came home to the normal world. You can't just return four months later and expect me to still be caught up in that drama!"

"Have you been sleeping with Tanner?" he asked coolly.

"What!" Reva was startled by the question. She had been involved trying to argue her side of the matter and here he was asking a totally unrelated question. "That's none of your business!"

"A simple yes or no will do, Reva," he told her quietly. "Have you been sharing his bed?"

"No!" she grated, not altogether certain why she was bothering to answer the impertinent question. "I've only known him a month, Josh!"

"You only knew me three days," he pointed out, the edge of his mouth turning upward.

"That's a terrible thing to say," she accused, flushing under the impact of his gaze.

"I'm trying to make a point. I knew the minute I saw you in the restaurant with him that you weren't sleeping with him," he told her with satisfaction.

"Then why bother to ask?" she hissed, and then spoiled the retort by tacking on, "How did you know?"

"I could tell by the way you smiled at him. Friendly and remote. And he didn't put up any fight at all when I took you away." Josh shrugged as if the case were open and shut. "But the reason I asked was to make you aware of something else. Tell me the truth, Reva Waring, has there been anyone since me?" The honey eyes suddenly narrowed and she felt his fingers harden briefly around her rib cage where he held her.

"I've . . . I've dated several people since I returned," she began quite bravely and winced as he gave her a slight impatient shake.

"That's not what I'm asking, little one, and you know it. Tell me, Reva!" The riverbed voice was still soft but very, very determined to have an answer.

"No," she muttered honestly. "It's none of your damn business, but, no, I haven't slept with anyone since I came back!"

"And there's been no one else for me since I put you on that plane," he told her, a slashing smile moving into place on his hard features. "You see? Even if you weren't conscious of it, you were waiting for me!"

"That's not true!" she blazed, alarmed at his deduction. "It just so happens that I don't engage routinely in affairs, and don't give me that line about there having been no one else for you, either! If that's the case it's only because you've been isolated in that jungle for four months. Which brings me right back to my initial statement. You've got some sort of fixation on me because I was the last woman you were with! As soon as you've had a chance to readjust to civilized society and meet people you'll feel differently. I'm surprised you haven't learned that about yourself by now. Surely this isn't the first time you've come back to the States on . . . on leave. . . ." Her words trailed off a little at the end because she wasn't absolutely certain what to call a mercenary's time off, and while Josh Corbett seemed a bit different from the way she had envisioned such men, she was fairly sure that was his occupation. What else could account for his presence in that terrible situation or for the way he'd been armed and at ease with the business of survival? Furthermore, he hadn't returned with her on the plane when he'd had the chance. Instead he'd walked back into the jungle with his weapons.

"Of course I've come and gone several times, little one," he smiled affectionately. "But I'm well aware my reaction to you was totally out of the ordinary. Do you think I normally go to all this trouble to track down women with whom I've shared a night or two?" He moved his hand along her thigh, shaped the contour of her waist, and then, with bold hunger, cupped a small breast. The lion eyes darkened as he bent his head and just before his mouth covered hers, he whispered hoarsely, "You're mine, Reva. I brought you safe out of that revolution and sent you home to wait for me. Now I've come to collect you!"

"Josh, listen to me . . ." Reva tried desperately, but it was too late. Her pleading words were silenced as his lips moved warmly on hers. She was clamped almost fiercely against his chest, helpless in the velvet-covered steel of his arms. His unsubtle, plundering mouth preyed hungrily on hers, forcing apart her lips and eagerly ravaging the honey behind them. She felt his tongue seek out hers and engage it immediately in a little duel of yin and yang, male and female.

Reva was profoundly aware of the explosive intent in

his hard body. He had tired of the arguments and explanations and attempts at reasoning. He told her with his hands and his lips and his possessive hold that he was here to claim the woman he felt belonged to him. Somehow, Reva told herself as the sensuous assault swept over her, she had thought she had more time. She had thought she could talk rationally to him for a while longer before giving up and throwing him out of the apartment.

But something had gone wrong. Here she was, cradled helplessly against him, every nerve aware of his questing, proprietary hands. She tried to protest and only a soft, kitten sound came from her throat. The tiny mew seemed to please him enormously and she felt herself gathered closer to his warmth and hardness.

The thing about Josh Corbett, Reva was reminded with stark clarity, was that he made love with total honesty. And she rediscovered what she had learned that night four months ago. For her there was nothing quite as captivating, nothing quite as dangerous as this man's utterly elemental approach to the act of love. It bypassed all the games and innuendoes of society, all the tricks and practiced seductions. For a woman like her there was nothing as incredibly seductive as this man's uncompromising and unhidden need. She had been a fool to let him come into the apartment.

"I don't think it's gratitude you're feeling tonight, little one," Josh husked against the lips he had lightly bruised. She heard the satisfaction in his voice and wanted to object but there was more than pure male pleasure in his words. There was desire and want and something else. Something gentle and almost pleading. Reva knew a sense of wonder that such a hard and seasoned survivor as Josh Corbett could plead for a woman's response. Almost without conscious volition, she lifted a hand and thrust her fingers through the graying hair of his temples and into the rich dark-brown mane beyond.

"Ah, Reva, Reva," he growled heavily, "I knew you couldn't have forgotten." And then his lips were moving to the corner of her mouth, dropping small, biting little kisses there and tracking upward to do the same at the corner of her faintly slanting blue-green eyes. As the tiny, stinging caresses descended, Reva's lids closed tightly and she felt a tremor of desire course the length of her body. She shifted her legs languidly as they lay across his thigh, arching her well-shaped feet in response to another faint shiver. One shiny black sandal came off and tumbled to the thick carpet, unnoticed.

Everything was different this time, Reva tried to tell herself as the spin of her emotions increased. This apartment was no abandoned hut with a dirt floor, she had not spent the day in fear for her life, and she had dined on fine veal, not stolen chicken. The man with her was wearing a wool suit instead of stained khakis and he didn't have a gun within arm's reach. And his face was clean shaven and smelled faintly of a tangy aftershave that combined potently with the natural male scent of his body.

Yes, everything was different but it didn't seem to matter one bit to the primitive, feminine core of her which ignored all the trappings and responded only to the masculine lures Josh was dispensing with a bold and generous hand.

"Josh, please," she began on a tiny, agitated wail, "I don't . . ."

"Honey," he interrupted thickly, his teeth tugging gently on her earlobe as his fingers worked to unbutton the small, elegant fastenings of the glimmering silk dress, "Don't ask me to go without you tonight! I've waited so long, dreamed about coming back to you so many sleepless nights! I couldn't bear not to satisfy my need of you now that you're finally in my arms. Tomorrow we can talk all you want."

His words came to a jagged halt and Reva heard his sharply indrawn breath as his fingers slipped inside the open bodice of the dress to palm the gentle curve of her breast. Nor was he the only one who reacted to the contact by sipping air. Reva gasped at the touch and turned her head into the material of his jacket. Instantly his mouth found the vulnerable nape of her neck and he kissed it as he toyed in increasing urgency with the hardening nipple he had captured between thumb and forefinger.

Reva trembled at the dual assault, striving frantically to regain some control over her own emotions before it was too late. Already her fingers were shaking slightly as she clutched the lapel of his jacket. The temptation to search out the buttons of his shirt, undo them, and seek the crisp, curling hairs of the smoothly muscled chest was rapidly becoming irresistible. For some reason Reva opened her drugged eyes and her gaze fell on the brilliant material of his tie. Grimly she focused on it.

"I've longed for the feel of your hands on me again, little Reva," Josh whispered with a sigh of eager anticipation. He moved and Reva thought he was going to get to his feet and carry her into the bedroom. She had to act now or it would be too late. Her rapidly disintegrating common sense warned her that if she let him go any farther she would be unable to stop him.

"Please, Josh," she managed thickly, making the crimson tie her whole point of reference. Something about its incongruity made it easier to concentrate on what she must say. "Let me go. You gave me your word not to

40

. . . to force me tonight, and if you go on that's how I'll regard it. The one thing I was sure of four months ago was that I could trust you. Don't destroy that now. . . ."

"Reva," he protested in a voice that tore along her nerve endings like sandpaper. "You'll want me as much as I want you. I swear it! Don't deny me the softness and the warmth I've been dreaming about all these months. I'm going to marry you as soon as possible, little one, I've told you that. You needn't be afraid I'll leave you alone again."

She heard the desperation and the blatant need in his words and her willpower almost collapsed. Who would have thought it would have been so difficult to fight the sheer intensity of his open and honest desire? Or that her own reaction to it would be so weakening? But that's all it was, Reva reminded herself forcibly, struggling to lift her head off his shoulder and meet his eyes. Desire. There could be nothing deeper or more important between herself and this man who lived and acted as if he'd grown up in the same alley as Xavier!

"Josh, listen to me," she pleaded, gazing up at him with anxious determination. She was supremely conscious of his physical superiority and the heat in his eyes as they swept over her disarrayed figure. She was completely at his mercy, lying across his lap like this, and she knew it. Her only weapons were words. "I'm truly sorry if you thought I was waiting patiently here in Portland to marry you. That's just not the way things are. I have a life of my own here and you're not a part of it. I shall always remember you and what you did for me, but I have no intention of furthering our relationship. We have absolutely nothing in common, Josh. Nothing at all!"

His hand stroked her hair as he continued to hold her close and the lion eyes looked searchingly down at her desperate expression. "Reva, honey, we have all we need

41

together. Don't worry about the little things. They're not important. Only you and I are important." There was a curiously soothing quality in his words, as if he were calming her, quieting her the way he had the night she'd awakened from the nightmare.

Reva shook her head. "No, Josh. Don't blow up out of all proportion that one night we had months ago. It was simply the result of the tension and fear I was going through at the time."

"Reva, it's not just that last night which made me so certain," Josh murmured gently. "There have been other nights and other women. I'm old enough not to read more into a situation than is there. You have to believe me, sweetheart. I'm a man, not a boy. I knew I wanted you the first day when I found you cornered in that kitchen, ready to use a knife against that bastard calling himself a revolutionary. You were so fierce and so gallant even though you didn't stand a chance against the gun he was wielding. For a split second after I'd taken care of him you held onto the knife and I could see in your eyes that you weren't sure but what I was just another one like the guerrilla had been. Then you calmly stepped over his body, put your hand in mine, and followed me out into the street. My God, Reva! I wanted to shout to the world that I'd found my woman at last. That she'd trusted me without asking any questions. Just put her hand in mine and walked out the door with me!"

Reva wanted to argue, to say something that made her action sensible. But the truth was she had taken the risk of trusting him without real evidence that he was any different from the man he'd shot in front of her. In many ways he'd looked vastly more dangerous than the young, violent guerrilla who'd attacked her. But she'd taken one look at the honey-brown eyes and known that everything was all right. This man would take care of her.

"You took care of me, Josh, and I'll never forget it, but . . ."

"I'm going to take care of you for the rest of our lives, honey," he promised simply. "You're mine."

"No," she said in a steadfast, utterly determined voice. "I don't belong to any man. What you're offering is not the sort of relationship I want, Josh. And soon enough you'll be going back to your . . . your job and forgetting all about me."

"You've really convinced yourself of that, haven't you?" he said after a moment's silence.

"Yes. It's the truth."

"And you'd send me away tonight? Leave me cold and hungry for you after all these months of waiting?" he went on in disbelieving wonder.

"Just because I made the mistake of sleeping with you once under very trying circumstances doesn't mean I'm foolish enough to repeat the error!"

"You're so sure it was a mistake?" he sighed, his face an unreadable mask as he watched her.

"Yes, Josh. I'm sure." She could feel the clash of wills begin to go in her favor. All she had to do was stay firm, Reva told herself. She kept very still in his lap, afraid to make a movement that might provoke him.

"You trusted me once, Reva," he began carefully.

"And I trust you now not to ask any more of me than I'm willing to give tonight," she interposed softly.

Without a word he tucked her head against his chest, under his chin. "I'd never hurt you, Reva, you must believe that." There was an ocean of feeling in the words, and against her will Reva felt them pull at her heart. She must not weaken!

43

"I believe it."

"But this matter has to be worked out, little one. You can't expect me to simply walk back out of your life now that I've found you again. I made up my mind the day I rescued you that you were going to belong to me. I can see you've built up some silly barriers in your head, but I can tear them down, and I will. But I'm going to resent every minute of the time that will be wasted teaching you the facts of life all over again," he added with a startlingly lighter note in his dark voice.

Reva raised her head in quick suspicion, nearly fetching up solidly against his chin. "Josh, I'm not just being stubborn! I know what I want and you'll only make things unnecessarily difficult if you persist in thinking there's something special in our acquaintance!" Her brows drew together in a frown as she wondered what he was planning.

"But fortunately," he went on with great calm, "I have plenty of time off to bring you to your senses. Where do I sleep, since I gather you're not going to offer me your bed?" He quirked an eyebrow at her in patient inquiry.

"You're not staying here, Josh!" There was a trace of desperation in her voice, Reva thought, trying frantically to get it under control.

"Yes, I am," he told her, setting her firmly on her feet and getting to his own. "I've already checked out of my hotel and I have no intention of hunting up another. Furthermore, I'm the man who saved your life four months ago. It seems to me the least you could do is put me up for the night!"

Reva stared at him, not quite certain how to take his new mood. He'd banked the fires of his passion with the iron will of a man who can exercise complete self-control when he chooses, but she wasn't sure what his next move was going to be. Before she could summon up further arguments, however, he was already striding toward the front door.

"Where are you going?" she demanded, annoyed with his strange actions. Xavier the cat lifted his head in casual question from across the room.

"I'm going to get my overnight bag," Josh explained to both of them, leaving the door open as he stepped out into the hall and knocked on the door of the adjacent unit.

"Josh, come back here!" Reva heard herself exclaim as she realized what he was doing. But it was too late. A moment later her neighbor Sandy opened the door. While Reva couldn't see her, she could hear her friend's voice quite clearly.

"Did you find her all right? Good. Here's the bag you asked me to hang onto for you. Perhaps we'll see you in the morning? Tom and I would love to get to know you better. After all, Reva's a great friend of ours. Give her my congratulations, will you? Tell her I'll see her tomorrow." Reva could almost picture Sandy's bright auburn head and attractive features as she peered around her door.

"Thank you and thank your husband for the directions to the restaurant. I had no trouble finding it at all," Josh said politely. A moment later the other door closed and Josh reappeared, bearing a battered leather bag which looked as though it had seen as much action as he had.

"Nice neighbors," he remarked laconically, kicking the door shut behind him and turning to throw the dead bolt. He tossed the leather bag down onto the carpet.

"Josh," Reva began boldly, "I won't have it. Do you understand? I don't have any obligation to provide you with a place to sleep tonight!"

"You owe me your life," he retorted with a wholly unexpected touch of brutality, coming toward her as he

45

stripped off his jacket. The lion eyes clashed with her blue-green gaze and it was Reva who glanced away.

"All right," she whispered, knowing she couldn't demand that he leave tonight, not if he was claiming a place to sleep as repayment for the way he'd saved her life. It was little enough she could do. And, besides, she wasn't at all sure how to get rid of him. Then there was Sandy and Tom next door. They'd surely hear the fracas if Reva tried to force her unwelcome visitor to leave. They would ask all sorts of questions. Questions she didn't feel up to answering tonight. In the morning she would explain everything to them. They would understand.

Head high, she faced Josh across the distance of the room. "The couch makes into a bed. I'll get some sheets. But this is it, Josh. In the morning you'll have to leave. Is that clear?"

"I hear you, little Reva," he half-smiled, halting a few feet away from her and watching her with such an intent look that she was suddenly afraid to say any more on the subject. She turned and went toward the hall closet to get the sheets and blankets.

Half an hour later Reva tumbled into her own bed, the bedroom door shut firmly behind her. For a long time she lay quietly thinking about the man sleeping on her couch. She had never tried too hard to imagine what a reunion between them might be like because she had firmly refused to contemplate that such a reunion was a genuine possibility. And now it had taken place and somehow it seemed vastly more difficult than she would have thought.

He would have to leave in the morning, she vowed to herself. He would *have* to leave. He was a hardened, weathered man but surely he couldn't be completely insensitive. He wouldn't stay when he realized she had no intention of being his 'dream' woman. And he would get over this strange fixation he'd developed about her. She wondered how often he had come out of the jungle in this sort of mood, and shivered. Were there other women scattered about the country who had felt the impact of his pent-up desire? Somehow she thought this situation was a little unique, just as he had claimed. Josh Corbett had no doubt known plenty of women, but she didn't see him as the type who vowed to marry each one with whom he had slept!

The thought brought a tiny smile to her face for the first time since she'd left the restaurant in his grasp, and Reva turned over on her side to settle down to sleep. She was going to have a job explaining all this to Sandy tomorrow!

It wasn't fair that the nightmare which had left her in peace for several weeks chose that night to return with a vengeance, but it did. Two hours after she'd closed her bedroom door Reva awakened in the darkness, perspiration soaking her green satin nightgown and her heart pounding. Had she cried out? Surely not, she thought, almost as terrified at the thought as she had been in the dream when she ran through the streets of the little town on the edge of the jungle, frantically searching for a place to hide. The sporadic gunfire cracked all around and the shouts and screams of a sleepy village caught up unwillingly in a revolution made her want to scream herself. But had she? She wished she'd let Xavier into her room before closing the door. More than once she'd comforted herself after the nightmare by hugging his warm, furry body close. But tonight she was alone in the room and the cat would have been unable to get inside.

Deliberately Reva forced herself to take deep, calming breaths. The dream had been stronger than in the past. A result of having the memories reinforced by Josh's presence? Perhaps. Whatever the reason, Reva seemed strangely unable to control the trembling which still wracked her body. The screams and the gunfire still rang in her head and she was always unable to find the safety she sought. In her dream she had clutched her passport exactly as she had that day, some instinct telling her to cling to it. But it could not stop a bullet or a man bent on rape and murder.

Damp and exhausted, Reva lay back against the pillows wondering over and over again if she had cried out during the dream. And then the door to her bedroom opened and she had her answer. Josh stood framed there, a large, dark, shadowy figure in the moonlight. Josh, who knew all about her nightmares.

CHAPTER THREE

"It's okay, Reva honey, I'm here." Josh's voice was soothing, calming, filled with the promise of protection. He came toward the bed, the dim light gleaming briefly on the broad expanse of his naked chest. He had taken the time to throw on his slacks, but that was all he was wearing.

Reva stared as he crossed the room on bare feet, making no sound on the pale, plush carpet. She knew she should order him out of her bedroom at once and she would, she vowed, as soon as she could be certain her voice wouldn't sound cracked. Her heart was slowly beginning to return to its normal rate but she still felt the aftermath of fear the dream always left behind.

"You are still having the nightmares, aren't you, sweetheart?" Josh murmured gently, sinking his heavy, smoothly muscled frame down onto the exotic Chinese print sheets and reaching immediately to scoop her up against him.

Reva wanted to object, pull away from the warmth and safety of his body, but somehow she couldn't seem to find the strength yet. She felt his hand in her hair, stroking through the thickness of it as it curved loose around her shoulders.

"I'm sorry, Josh," she whispered, "I didn't mean to disturb you. Just a dream. Did I scream or something?"

Almost unwillingly she began to relax under the quieting feel of his hands.

"You called my name," he explained, as if it were the most natural thing in the world that she had done so. She felt the hand holding her against his chest as it burned warmly through the thin material of her nightgown. "And I'm here to take care of you. Everything's all right, Reva. You can relax and let me hold you until the dream is completely gone." There was a pause and then he added with a touch of wry amusement, "At least your instincts are still sound, even if you have managed to convince yourself you don't belong to me!"

"No, Josh," Reva tried to protest weakly, "it was only a dream! Probably caused by seeing you again and having all the old memories brought back!" That wasn't altogether fair, she realized, but she needed some defense. The heat and strength of him were becoming much too enticing and she knew it but still couldn't find the will to pull away. A few more minutes, she told herself reassuringly, and then she would disengage herself from the comforting embrace.

"Does being here in my arms bring back *all* the memories, Reva?" he asked deliberately. "Do you remember what happened after you awoke from the nightmare that first time? How you huddled against me like this and I held you until your pulse had slowed and your breathing was normal and the fear had gone from your body?" His voice was strangely, comfortingly hypnotic, Reva thought dimly, realizing she was far more vulnerable now than she had been earlier. The aftereffects of the dream, the slightly otherworldly feeling provided by the moonlight, and the sheer impact of Josh's presence were a potent combination. She shivered again but this time it wasn't from fear.

"Josh," she husked against his chest, turning her face

50

into his shoulder, "I don't want to remember the rest. I've tried so hard to forget."

"I can see that, honey, but it wasn't meant to be forgotten," he told her, his lips in her hair. "What we had four months ago was too special, too important."

"No." But the single negative was almost a whimper and Reva was keenly aware of Josh's fingers lying alongside her breast. Her feet twisted in the sheets as she shifted slightly in a vague effort to free herself. But when his hands tightened she stopped trying and allowed herself to be held.

"Yes," he corrected firmly, with total conviction, "and I'm going to prove it to you. I'm going to break through all these silly defenses you've spent your time putting up during the past few months and show you that the only thing that really counts is us. Together. Can't you see how you cry out for me when you're having bad dreams and see how you cuddle against me when I soothe you? Doesn't that tell you anything, honey?" His hands moved gently over her, but Reva was suddenly aware that there was no passion in them, only an offer of comfort. She settled instinctively closer even as she tried to marshal her arguments.

"Josh, please don't make more out of this than it deserves." Automatically she raised her head to meet his eyes but when her chin came up, he bent his head and took her lips quite gently and inevitably.

"I think your problem," he murmured against her mouth, "is that you've overintellectualized the whole matter. A woman like you should trust her emotions more." His lips moved slowly, invitingly, sensuously on hers.

The hands which had held no threat of passion only a few seconds earlier were stirring along her body in a different way. But Reva was trapped. She had relaxed too much, accepted the calming touch and let the soothing words wash over her when she should have been laughing off the dream and telling Josh to leave. Now it was quite suddenly too late and she knew it as surely as she had known in the restaurant that there was no chance Josh would fail to spot her in the crowd. Since she had first seen him that evening there had been an inner knowledge that it would eventually end like this.

Without any further mental arguments or lectures, Reva stopped fighting both herself and Josh. It was so much easier to simply let him take over for a time. The need to feel his strength enveloping hers and know the hard leanness of his body once again was too much. She trembled beneath the touch of his hands and he felt it, responded to it.

With a kind of wonder Reva touched the curling hair on his chest. Gingerly at first and then with increasing fascination and urgency she began toying with the dark crispness of it, searching out the male nipples and caressing them even as Josh found the tips of her breasts. Feeling as if she had temporarily suspended the rational portion of her mind, Reva arched deliciously, languidly against Josh's hand and reveled in the groan she elicited from him. The strong fingers which had begun by gently teasing her nipples turned more passionate and demanding, providing almost a pleasure-pain as she responded.

"Oh, Josh," Reva breathed, her senses beginning to swim as pure sensation took over to govern her reactions. "I'd almost forgotten what it was like."

"Had you, little one?" he grated on the skin of her throat. "It seems I came back just in time." He slid her nightgown down to her waist and with a small moan of undisguised desire lowered his head to let his lips replace his fingers on her breast. Gently Reva was lowered back against the pillows and Josh sprawled heavily across her, trapping her restless legs with his own.

"I told you earlier that I had never wanted a woman as much as I wanted you that night before I put you on the plane, but since then it's only gotten more intense for me," he husked thickly between a series of small, stinging kisses that seemed to flick her skin like a tiny whip. "Tonight I want you more than ever!"

Reva shivered at the raw sexual need in his words, thrilling to the increasingly intimate touch of his fingers as they traced erotic patterns over the curve of her hip and around to the delicious, sensitive softness of her inner thigh. She could no longer deny to herself that there was something unique in Josh's lovemaking for her. Something that, temporarily at least, made everything else seem unimportant. A distant part of Reva's mind was aware that she was succumbing to an uncontrollable desire that made no sense and should be fiercely stamped out. But tonight there was absolutely nothing she could do or wanted to do to stop it.

"Tell me what you're feeling, my sweet, passionate little Reva," Josh demanded in a low growl of urgency. "I want to know if you're half as crazy as I am right now!"

"I must be crazy, Josh," she admitted, curving her hips upward in an effort to feel his hand more intimately. "Nothing makes sense tonight. I only know I want you, need you!"

"I can feel your need, little one," he assured her with a masculine satisfaction that should have annoyed her but didn't. She was too far gone in her sensual world to think about the implications of her surrender. "You're so warm and soft and passionate. You were made for me, Reva Waring, and only a complete fool would throw away a gift

53

from the gods. I may be many things, but I'm not a fool!" His hand probed the very heart of her desire and Reva gasped in response, her breath beginning to come in quick, sharp pants.

"Oh, yes!" she cried out softly, arching closer, clinging to his shoulders in an effort to draw him more tightly against her slenderness. "Oh, Josh, please, please . . ." Reva's eyes were closed against the outside world as her body focused only on the pleasure and need and desire it was experiencing at this man's hands.

His mouth returned to hers, his tongue invading with a forceful demand that allowed only response, not resistance, assuming Reva had still been capable of resistance. She was more than willing to give him the reactions he seemed to crave. Her fingers dug into the muscles of his back and trailed down to his waist, circling and seeking the sensitive areas, delighting in each newly discovered one. There was a deep excitement in making love to Josh, Reva acknowledged, because he kept back nothing of his own response. He made no secret of his pleasure in her touch and that communication seemed to drive Reva's own level of response higher and higher.

Unable to restrain herself any longer, Reva turned more closely than ever into the heat of Josh's body, her fingers fumbling with the clasp of his slacks. She was impatient with the barrier of his clothes, wanting only to complete the inevitable union.

"My sweet, soft, Reva," Josh grated gently, his hand possessing the dampening, secret part of her. "I knew it wouldn't be long before you remembered everything about the way it was between us. You'll be mine legally, little one, just as soon as I can arrange it. In the morning I'll take care of everything. . . ."

Blearily, Reva's love-drugged mind sought to comprehend exactly what Josh was saying and the instinct which had warned her earlier in the evening not to surrender reawakened. With Josh such a surrender this time could very well be final. She would not have another four months alone to reconsider her actions. And he was all wrong for her! She must remember that!

"Josh, no," she managed, fighting desperately for control over herself and the situation. How could she have let things go so far? It was all the fault of that nightmare. It weakened her so terribly and Josh was so warm and comforting.

"Yes, sweetheart," he muttered with a small hint of ferocity. "It was meant to be for us. You must understand that. I made you mine four months ago and now I must have what belongs to me!" His mouth burned along her shoulder, his tongue exploring the skin as if he was tasting her.

"No marriage, Josh!" she wailed helplessly, her head moving in a restless denial. But how could she deny the feel of him against her?

"Reva, honey," he said slowly, his voice husky but carrying a new seasoning of steel. "I haven't come back after all this time just to take you to bed."

Reva knew a touch of incipient hysteria. Every woman longed to hear such reassurance from the man who claimed a lover's rights. But this was the wrong man and she should know better than to give him such rights regardless of what he promised for the future. In fact, it would be better for all concerned if she granted him a physical surrender only and denied him anything else. But that wasn't like her! She couldn't sleep with a man she didn't love. But hadn't she done exactly that four months ago? The blunt truth made her cringe inwardly.

For a long moment there was a tense silence and Reva

had the impression Josh was struggling to gain control of himself. His hands stopped moving on her body and a traitorous part of her wanted to cry out at the loss. But her own mental self-control seized at the respite to try and reestablish normal defenses. Reva drew long, steadying breaths, her eyes closed.

"With very little effort," Josh murmured deeply at last, "I could take you tonight, couldn't I, Reva? Admit that much at least, honey. You were more than ready to surrender in my arms, weren't you?"

Reva refused to open her eyes and meet the demand she knew she would see in his face so close to her own. It was the truth. Why not verbally give him that much satisfaction? He knew it, anyway.

She nodded her head mutely and was rewarded by being pulled more tightly against his chest. Still she kept her eyes fiercely shut.

"Before I met you, Reva, that's all the surrender I ever wanted from a woman," he said deliberately, meaningfully. "But from you that's not good enough. Do you begin to comprehend, little Reva?"

Reva, the elemental female in her understanding all too well the completeness of the surrender he asked, chilled.

"Josh, that's all there can be between us. We're so different . . ." she started desperately, striving to make him understand.

When she finally opened her eyes it was to see the grim line of his mouth tighten still further as did his hold on her.

"You're blinding yourself to the truth, Reva, because you're afraid to trust your emotions to such an extent. But it's not going to do you any good, sweetheart, because I'm going to seduce you completely, wear you down and wear

56

you out. I swear to God I'll find the key to unlock the door you've closed on me!"

Reva's eyes widened in shock at the rasping intensity and determination in his voice. "But you already . . . I mean, tonight you could have done that, seduced me. A moment ago I wouldn't have stopped you. . . ." Her voice trailed off in bewilderment.

Josh shaped the line of her throat with his fingertips, pausing at the pulse in the hollow. His gaze enmeshed hers so that she couldn't have escaped if she'd tried.

"Don't get me wrong, sweetheart," he drawled in a tone which Reva thought contained something suspiciously akin to humor. "I shall be more than delighted to have your physical surrender. All I'm saying is that it's not enough. I want all the trust back. The trust you had in me four months ago. And I want the compassion and the need. I want to make my home with you, Reva Waring. It's time I had a home like other men. I may not deserve it, but I'm going to get it if it's the last thing I do!"

"That's . . . that's not what you and I have together," Reva heard herself say almost harshly. "I'll admit that physically you and I are . . ." She hesitated, flushing as she searched for the right word.

"Compatible?" he suggested with a mocking dryness in his voice.

"Well, yes," she defended vigorously. "It's called desire, Josh, and it can happen to two people. You know that. You told me a few minutes ago that it was all you'd ever asked for in a woman."

"If it were all I wanted from you, I would have taken you tonight," he smiled gently.

"It's all I have to give you," she snapped. "Or rather, it's all I *had* to give you! I find I'm quite recovered from my nightmare now! In the future I shall have a much

57

firmer grip on myself, I assure you." Reva let anger whip her defenses firmly back into place. She would be far more careful around this man, she promised herself grimly.

He shook his head as if finding her touchingly amusing. "I'll be able to have your physical response anytime I want it, little Reva, and I shall probably want it frequently, if only to console myself while I wait for you to come to your senses and take me in."

"No, you will not!" she declared furiously. "I have more self-control than you seem to think. It was only that nightmare which made me weak tonight. I . . . I would have been glad of anyone's comfort!"

The lion gaze narrowed and Reva had the impression she might have been a little too rash. An odd sensation of anxiety raced through her as she waited for his response.

"Don't say things like that, honey," he ordered in a deep, heavy voice that seemed to vibrate through the room. "There isn't going to be anyone else in your life. I'm home and I'm claiming what's mine. For everyone's sake, don't drag another man into this. I'm going to do my best to be patient with you and work out all the problems you're having about our relationship, but if you try using another man in your resistance tactics I won't be responsible for the results!"

Reva blinked uncertainly at the clear warning in his words. It was the first time this evening she'd seen the glint of the steel she knew was just below the surface of the man.

"I'm not going to alter my whole life for you, Josh," she ground out coldly. "Saving my neck doesn't give you the right to come back and assume you can do as you like with me!"

"Yes, it does, sweetheart," he told her calmly, irrefutably.

"How can you say that!" she stormed, infuriated.

He shrugged mildly. "It's the truth. I want you and I'm going to make you admit you want me. If there's one thing I've learned in this life, Reva, it's that a man has to go after the important things. And you're very, very important to me."

"For how long, Josh?" she challenged bravely. "Until you get bored and go off on another assignment somewhere else in the world?"

"I've learned not to spend valuable energy on passing fancies, honey. I'm not going to exert all this patience and effort on someone I only want in my bed for a month or two! Give me some credit, Reva, I'm thirty-eight years old. I've learned a few things about myself and others."

"And you think you want me as a wife!" she scoffed, wondering silently at the prickle of intrigue that she was experiencing. One thing could safely be said about Josh Corbett and that was that he was very different from any other man she had ever known. It stood to reason his approach to getting a a wife would also be different. It was proving as deliberate and overwhelming as the rest of his actions.

"I'm ready for a home and a woman of my own, little one, and I'm going to get it."

"Josh, be reasonable," Reva urged gently, her heart suddenly going out to this man who had convinced himself that he wanted what other men his age had and was going to take it. "Your . . . your job isn't exactly conducive to a good home life. You must see that." She felt him tense at her words.

"What's wrong with my career?" he asked, sounding startled. She wondered that he had never questioned his own brutal line of work. "I can support a wife!" He sounded as if he'd taken offense at the implication.

Reva took a deep breath, managing to free one of her

wrists at last. She looked into Josh's now perplexed expression and sighed. "People who fight other people's wars for them couldn't possibly make good husbands. Admit it, Josh. What you want is for men who live normal lives and have normal jobs."

"Other people's wars!" He looked positively astounded. Levering himself up into a sitting position and bracing himself against the headboard with one hand he glared down into her tightly drawn face. "What the hell are you talking about, Reva Waring!"

Reva bit her lip, not having expected him to try and deny his means of livelihood. Whatever else he might be, Josh was honest. Or at least she had always thought him so. "It was pretty obvious what you were doing down there in South America, Josh," she said quietly, sitting up and adjusting the nightgown back into position. She used the small action as an excuse not to meet his eyes. She knew he was getting angry. But he reached out and snagged her chin, forcing her full attention. The grim set of his face made her swallow nervously.

"You think," he began slowly, as if not quite able to comprehend the extent of her stupidity, "that I'm some kind of damn mercenary?"

"Aren't you?" she replied in a small, flat voice.

"No!" he slung back instantly, clearly incensed. "God in heaven, woman, whatever gave you that idea?"

"It . . . it seemed obvious, Josh," she murmured a little desperately, thoroughly confused herself now. "Everything about you . . ." Her hand waved in a vague little motion as she let the sentence falter. "The first time I saw you, you were carrying that rifle and you looked as if you'd been doing it half your life. And you didn't even pause when you shot that creature who was attacking me.

You seemed so hard and tough. Oh, Josh, what was I to think?"

"You could have asked me!" he growled.

"How do you ask a man if he's a professional killer!" she blazed. But a strange sense of hope was flickering alive deep inside. Firmly she stamped it out. Even if this man wasn't what she had thought, he still was not the one for her.

"Reva, you little idiot, it never occurred to me that you thought I was a professional mercenary. I thought I told you at one point that I was in the country doing business with its government when that uprising broke out." Josh shook his head in exasperation.

"I thought that was just a polite way of saying you worked for the ruling faction," Reva mumbled, beginning to be embarrassed by the misunderstanding. She could feel the heat in her cheeks and was glad of the darkness. Josh's fingers still clamped her face in a viselike grip, though, and it was impossible to turn away.

"Reva," he began with clearly limited patience, "as the senior company man on the scene when the revolutionaries attempted to overthrow the government, it was my responsibility to oversee the evacuation of my firm's personnel. It was in the course of that process that I acquired the weapons. They were given to me by a military officer because he couldn't spare the men needed to protect our people. I got our personnel out and then decided to stay behind to protect my company's interests. There was talk of nationalizing all foreign-owned businesses. I had some contacts in the government and thought that if I stayed on the scene I would have a better chance of preventing a government or a revolutionary takeover of the firm's assets. That's all there was to it. I was keeping a low profile until matters cooled down when I got word that there was an American woman trapped in one of the outlying villages. I came looking for you and found you." He shrugged his massive shrug.

Reva unclenched her unconsciously compressed fingers, a curious wave of relief rolling over her at learning the truth. "I'm glad, Josh," she said simply, meaning it. She decided not to press him for all the details, such as how he'd done such a good job of keeping them both alive. She had the notion most modern U.S. business firms didn't include that in management training.

"Reva, honey," he went on more mildly as she lowered her lashes against the perceptive gleam in his honey eyes, "Was this matter of believing I was a mercenary the reason you didn't think I'd come back for you? Is that why you were so frightened when I talked of marriage?"

"It was definitely one of the reasons," she admitted dryly. "You'll have to agree that the prospect of marrying a man who is only at home when he's resting between campaigns isn't a very thrilling one!"

"No, I can see where it wouldn't be," he said, and she could hear the new thread of humor in his voice. He seemed to be experiencing a sense of relief, too, she realized. "Well, I'm glad we got that out in the open," he added, and then, quite carelessly, as if it were all settled: "How soon will you marry me, honey? I've got a month off before I have to be back at work."

"Josh!" Reva stared at him, startled. "Nothing has changed! I'm very glad you're not . . . what I thought you were, but that doesn't make any real difference between us. We're still two entirely different people and we both lead different lives. In spite of what you think, we know virtually nothing about each other."

His look hardened perceptibly and he reached over to grab a pillow which he stuffed behind himself. "Don't tell me," he grated, sprawling disgustedly back against the headboard, "that I'm right where I was earlier this evening. Square one!" He appeared thoroughly short tempered about the matter, Reva thought worriedly.

"I can't imagine what gave you the impression that the only thing standing in the way of a marriage between us was my opinion of your supposed career!" she snapped a bit wildly. "I've told you, there are several reasons."

"We *are* back to square one," he sighed, closing his eyes tightly for a moment and rubbing the bridge of his nose in a slow, massaging action that suddenly made him look very tired. "Why did I have to go and fall for a stubborn, idiotic little female who can face an armed guerrilla like a cornered cat but who can't face her own emotions with any courage at all!"

"I am not being cowardly!" Reva hissed.

"It's all right, honey," Josh told her, reaching out a large hand to pat her on the head in a totally incongruous action that enraged her. "I knew what was best for you back in that jungle and I know what's best for you here. I'll take care of you." He yawned, raising a fist to cover his mouth.

"You haven't 'fallen' for me," Reva argued forcefully. "It's only that you've spent the past four months isolated in that awful little country. It was only natural that you'd concentrate on the last woman you'd . . . you'd been with. You'll get over the fixation once you've had a chance to readjust. Believe me!"

He blinked, looking rather sleepy. "What makes you such an authority on my reactions? You don't even understand your own!"

"I'm merely exercising some common sense, Josh!" she yelped furiously.

"So we revert to plan A which I outlined a little while

ago," he sighed, leaning deeper into the pillows behind him and watching her with a somewhat owlish expression. "The wearing-down routine."

"That's nonsense!"

"I agree, but you seem to be lacking in sense, so we'll try it the other way. Actually, it might be rather interesting. I've never set out to completely seduce a woman. Getting them into bed always seemed enough before I met you." He yawned again, ignoring Reva's fierce look. "But I think I'll have to start the project in the morning. I know this doesn't sound particularly romantic, but I'm exhausted. I've spent the past few months working day and night to salvage my company's holdings in that godforsaken country, and as soon as I could get away I came straight here to Portland where I was again obliged to work day and night tracking you down. I'm tired, Reva. Do you mind if we continue this brilliant conversation in the morning?"

But he wasn't really asking for agreement, apparently. Josh had already made his decision, Reva thought ruefully, watching as he closed his eyes and turned over on his stomach. He calmly went to sleep beside her, the slow, even pattern of his breathing telling her he wasn't playing games. She waited a few minutes, staring down at his broad, tanned back in mingled astonishment and disgust, and then, not having the heart to try and kick him out of bed, she dragged the quilt up over his shoulders. He was tired, she thought wonderingly, thinking of how indefatigable he had seemed during those three days in South America. He must have been through a lot since then, she told herself. And she had already told him he could stay the night. What did it matter whether he slept in here or out on the couch?

It wasn't her decision to let him stay in her bed that

surprised Reva, it was the temptation she experienced to stay beside him. For a long, intriguing moment she sat amid the covers and toyed with the notion of simply slipping down alongside his lean warmth. Then the rational side of her mind took over. Matters had come perilously close to disaster once tonight when she'd practically thrown herself into his arms. She'd been downright lucky he'd convinced himself he wanted her mental as well as physical surrender. It would be stupid to have him wake up beside her and decide he'd take what he could get, after all!

Very carefully Reva slipped from the bed, adjusting the covers once more over the large man lying half tangled in her sheets. Then she padded silently out of the room, closing the door softly behind her. In the living room she found Xavier curled in the middle of the sofa bed and she smiled at him as she got under the covers.

"Did you have a nice conversation out here with my guest, cat?" she asked politely, propping herself on her elbow and slowly stroking the large animal's thick gray fur. He opened his eyes sleepily to let her know he heard her and then pressed himself cozily against the warmth of her leg. His right ear, which had been chewed rather badly in a long-forgotten fight, twitched absently.

"I thought the two of you might get along quite well," Reva went on softly, her eyes on the city lights which sparkled below her eighteenth-floor apartment. "There's something about that man which reminds me of you, Xavier. He told me he's not what I thought he was but I still have the feeling he's been through a lot. Like you, he's tough and he's carrying some scars, even if they're not visible. And now he's decided he wants a home." Reva sighed gently, settling back against the pillow. "I'm grateful to him, Xavier. But you can't marry a man out of

65

gratitude. And even if he's not a mercenary, it doesn't take much insight to realize he's not at all the sort of man I want for a husband. I'm sure the only thing we have in common is that time we spent in South America. No, tomorrow I'll tell him he has to leave," she concluded decisively. With that thought firmly etched in her mind, Reva turned on her side and went to sleep.

Saturday morning dawned cloudy and wet. The Portland sky drizzled rain down onto a city long accustomed to such weather and Reva awoke with a long, luxurious stretch. It took a moment to realize she wasn't in her own bed and then her memory snapped back into focus. Josh Corbett had returned and this morning she had to find a way to get rid of him. She didn't want to risk any further repetitions of last night's near surrender. With a determined, energetic motion Reva threw back the covers, ignoring Xavier's protests at being summarily awakened, and headed for the bathroom. A brisk shower was called for before she tackled her unwanted guest, Reva thought.

The shower refreshed her considerably, as had the night's sleep. Reva emerged in her bathrobe, certain that Josh, whom she remembered distinctly as being an early riser, would already be up and about. Indeed, she was mildly surprised he hadn't awakened first. But, then, he had seemed genuinely exhausted last night, she reminded herself. She hesitated outside her bedroom door for a moment, listening for sounds of activity within, and frowned when she heard none. Reluctant to walk in as long as Josh still occupied the bed, Reva decided to forego dressing for the moment and headed, instead, for the kitchen. It seemed reasonable enough to provide him some breakfast before she told him to leave. He'd certainly provided her with enough meals in the past!

She frowned as she peered into the nearly empty refrig-

66

erator. A couple of grapefruit and some eggs were about all that looked appealing. Josh would be hungry, she thought wryly. He would probably be expecting something on the order of bacon and eggs and toast or stacks of hotcakes. Well, he would have to make do with what she normally ate, although she supposed she could double his portions of poached eggs and grapefruit.

She puttered around the efficient little kitchen for a few minutes, preparing coffee and cutting the grapefruit. Then she paused once again to listen for sounds from behind her door. Nothing.

Growing vaguely curious, Reva walked to the still-shut door and raised a hand to knock very gently. There was no response. Perhaps she should let him sleep, she thought. But surely he'd had enough rest by now. It was getting late. She knocked once again, louder. This time when there was no answer, she called his name.

"Josh?"

This time there was an answering thud from within. It sounded as if her alarm clock had been pushed off the bedside table. Growing somewhat worried, Reva called Josh's name once more and this time when there was no answer she pushed open the door, a quelling frown in place in case he was playing some sort of game with her.

But Josh didn't look at all as though he were playing games. He didn't look as though he could even attempt the effort. Reva stared in consternation at his large form huddled, obviously shivering, beneath the weight of the quilt, the bedspread, and a couple of spare blankets he'd located at the foot of the bed.

"Josh! What's wrong?" Hurrying into the room, Reva nearly tripped over the alarm clock which was lying on the floor, pushed there by an outflung hand that now trailed over the edge of the bed. He stirred at the sound of her

67

voice, opening the honey-colored eyes just wide enough to regard her balefully through two narrow slits.

"It's all right, Reva," he mumbled heavily. "I'll be up soon. Give me a few more minutes." His eyes closed as if the effort had been too much. The outflung hand rose to his forehead. "My head's killing me," he muttered.

"You're ill!" Reva exclaimed.

He opened his eyes and regarded her once again through the slitted lashes. "Something I picked up a few years ago on a trip to South America. It hits me once in a while." He winced painfully. "I'll be over it in a few days. Nothing for it but aspirin and rest."

A few days! Reva stood beside the bed, staring nonplused at the man in it. She knew immediately that all her plans for getting rid of Josh Corbett by that afternoon had just vanished in a puff of smoke. She couldn't throw the man who had saved her life out of her apartment when he was in this condition!

CHAPTER FOUR

"Reva, honey, I want you to know I'm sorry about last night," Josh began half an hour later as he sat propped up in bed picking unenthusiastically at poached eggs and grapefruit. He looked up with a bleak, rueful expression to meet her eyes as she sat at the foot of the bed, Xavier in her lap. "I know I must have embarrassed the hell out of you at that restaurant and Lord knows what you must have thought of me later!" He shook his head and swallowed a bite of the rosy grapefruit carefully. He'd explained that one of the symptoms of his complaint included a sore throat. "All I can say in my own defense is that I was probably coming down with this bug yesterday and went a little crazy. The main part of the fever hit me last night. I certainly was looking forward to seeing you again, but I sure didn't intend to make all those nutty demands about marriage!"

Reva smiled a little uncertainly, freeing Xavier, who had taken a notion to leave the comfort of her lap in favor of investigating the contents of Josh's breakfast tray. She watched him affectionately as he padded across the quilt, her hands idly brushing cat hair from her expensive designer slacks. Gray cat hair discovered at various location around the apartment and on her person had become a fact of life since Xavier had moved in. Reva accepted it philosophically and merely brushed it off when she found it on the cushions of the chinoiserie-style furniture or on her clothes. She had gotten dressed before she cooked Josh's breakfast and, in addition to the well-made camel slacks, she wore a soft, plush velour pullover striped in deep jewel tones. The sun-washed hair was brushed into a loose curve around her shoulders, held back over one ear by a cloisonné comb, and her bold frames were perched aggressively on her nose. She peered consideringly at her guest through the lenses and her smile widened.

"I don't know whether to be offended or not!" she chuckled, feeling vastly more relaxed around the large man in her bed now that he was meekly sidelined with the strange malady. "You mean you haven't spent the past four months dreaming of coming back here and forcing me into marriage?"

He groaned feelingly and she giggled at his rueful expression. "Don't tease me, Reva," he pleaded. "I feel bad enough as it is! I came here to Portland to spend some of my time off with someone I'd come to consider a very close friend. I expect I was a little upset by having to waste half a week locating you and then finding you out on a date. Typical male reaction compounded by the beginnings of a fever. Forgive me?" The honey-colored eyes watched her with genuine pleading and the hard line of his mouth was twisted wryly.

"Of course I do, Josh," Reva relented at once, thinking how harmless he looked this morning compared to the returning warrior of last night. She had really let her imagination run wild all those months ago. The thought made her bite her lip and she realized she had an apology of her own to make. "Do you forgive me for thinking you were some sort of cutthroat mercenary?" she asked with a self-deprecating smile.

He returned the expression and nodded his head. Then he raised a hand to the back of his neck as if the motion had escalated the headache. "Damn!" he muttered, "I feel weak as a kitten. No offense, Xavier," he added to the cat, who was politely eyeing the remains of a poached egg. "I'm sorry to make a nuisance out of myself, Reva. It's very decent of you to let me stay here while I recover after the way I behaved!"

"Well, you can't go to a hotel in your present condition. You could fall and hurt yourself during a dizzy spell like the one you had a few minutes ago coming back from the bathroom. Besides, how would you eat?" Reva pointed out logically.

"Room service?" he suggested weakly.

"Nonsense. You need good food when you're ill, not greasy french fries and hamburgers, which is probably what you'd order," Reva contradicted briskly, getting to her feet to tidy the covers around him. "Do you want some hot tea with lemon and honey? Very soothing on the throat," she asked invitingly as she patted the quilt into place.

"Sounds wonderful," he agreed, raising his eyes to meet hers. He looked very thankful, she thought. "You have all the makings of a good nurse," he told her. "My throat feels like steel wool. Maybe I'll move out onto the couch in the living room. You're not going to want to sit in here by my bed all day and I would like to talk to you. Aren't you curious to know how things turned out after you left on the DC-3 that morning?" he began, and then interrupted his question with a muttered oath. "Xavier, you thief!"

"What happened?" Reva asked, turning around to glance at the cat, who was calmly swishing a pink tongue around his whiskers.

"He got the last of the egg when I wasn't looking," Josh grumbled. "Haven't you taught this beast any manners?"

Reva chuckled fondly. "Unfortunately, I didn't have Xavier from kittenhood. By the time he adopted me he was fully grown and had picked up any number of bad habits living in alleys. He tries to put on a façade of politeness and civilized behavior but underneath he's still an alley cat."

"Takes what he wants and to hell with the rest of the world?" Josh growled.

"Something like that."

"I'm surprised you tolerate him," Josh noted mildly, glaring at the cat. "He doesn't seem to fit in with your life-style." He swept a hand out to indicate the chic oriental-style furniture, the beautiful apartment, and the rich off-white carpeting. Then he slanted a strange look up at Reva, who was closing a closet door she had left open. She felt his glance and looked back at him over her shoulder.

"He doesn't," she shrugged. "But something about him appeals to me and besides, I'm not at all sure I could get rid of him if I tried." She walked back to the edge of the bed and frowned thoughtfully down at Josh. "Are you sure you want to move out into the living room? Perhaps you should be sleeping."

"Believe me, I've had this bug often enough in the past to know how it's going to react. Sore throat, headache, fever in the beginning and occasional dizziness, plus a general weakness. It will run its course in a few days and I'll be fine. In the meantime there's nothing to do but rest and I can do that as well out on the couch."

"If you're sure . . ."

"I'm sure."

Reva arranged quilts and pillows on the dark red couch, assisting her patient out to his new bed when all was ready.

Xavier followed along, jumping up to nap at Josh's feet when he was reestablished. She fixed Josh the honey-and-lemon tea, and agreed to a game of cards when he proposed it.

Reva was in the middle of laying down her third winning hand in a row when the phone rang. She picked up the receiver of the red instrument, which matched the couch in color, and automatically said hello, her mind still on the gin rummy game. She was deliberately keeping an eye on Josh, who had shown signs of being willing to cheat, although it hadn't done him any good so far.

"Bruce!" she exclaimed in surprise as she recognized the voice on the other end. "Yes, that's right, you said you'd call!" She smiled with pleasure, her eyes on Josh, who glanced up with a frown as she spoke the other man's name. The frown cleared almost immediately, however, and he went back to studying his hand.

"Everything's fine, Bruce," Reva said in reassuring response to her caller's first question. "Poor Josh has come down with some sort of recurrent illness that he gets occasionally, though, and I'm putting him up for a couple of days."

"Did he ask you to do that?" Bruce demanded on the other end of the line.

"Oh, no," Reva laughed. "He was all set to move into a hotel but he couldn't possibly get good care there."

"I see," Bruce remarked a little stiffly. "I'm a bit surprised you're willing to be so kind to him after the way he behaved last night."

"He apologized for all that," Reva explained. "And he is an old acquaintance, Bruce. I can't throw him out into the street. I owe him a favor." She thought Josh tensed briefly as she said the last words, but he didn't look up.

"What sort of favor?" Bruce asked suspiciously.

"I'll tell you all about it some day," Reva promised, not wanting to go into the subject.

There was a silence on the other end of the line for a moment and then Bruce went on a bit aggressively. "Do you still want to go to that concert Sunday evening?"

"I most certainly do," Reva said at once. "I wouldn't miss it for the world. You know that!"

"I wasn't sure if you might feel you had to baby-sit," he grumbled.

"I think Josh can stay by himself tomorrow evening," Reva laughed. "What time shall I expect you?"

"I'll pick you up around seven o'clock," Bruce told her, sounding slightly mollified.

"I'll be looking forward to it." She said her good-byes and hung up the phone.

"Tanner?" Josh asked curtly as Reva resumed her seat on the hassock beside the couch. He kept his attention on the new hand of gin he had just dealt.

"That's right. He was worried about me after watching you drag me out of the restaurant last night," Reva smiled, considering her cards carefully.

"If he was all that worried he shouldn't have let me do it," Josh said coolly, selecting a discard. "I sure as hell wouldn't have let some stranger walk up and haul my woman off into the night!"

Reva lifted one brow quellingly behind her glasses. "I'm hardly Bruce's 'woman,' Josh," she commented with a caustic note in her voice. "I was his date for the evening and I chose to leave of my own free will. I hate scenes and you looked very much as if you were prepared to make one!"

Josh winced. "Sorry," he mumbled. "I've already apologized for that. But just the same, it seems to me if he really cared for you he should have been a little more, uh, forceful in looking after you!"

Reva lifted one shoulder negligently. "Bruce knows I'm capable of looking after myself."

There was a pause while they continued the play of the cards and then Josh said quietly, "Are you really considering marrying the man?"

"Yes." She selected a card from the discard pile, frowning as she added it to her hand. For some reason she was glad of the small excuse not to meet Josh's inquiring gaze.

"Why?"

"Why?" She did look up at that. "For a lot of reasons, naturally." Josh's eyes were curiously remote and detached as they studied her.

"Tell me about him, Reva," he suggested easily.

"What do you want to know?"

"What you see in him. Why you think you want to marry him. I'll admit I'm interested. I feel a little protective of you, I suppose, after that time we had together."

Reva relaxed slightly, a small, warm smile lifting the corners of her mouth. "That's sweet of you, Josh," she said, meaning it. "But you needn't worry about me. I know what I'm doing. Bruce is perfect for me."

"In what way?" Josh asked calmly.

"Well, he's considerate, intelligent, well mannered, and shares many of the same interests I do. Furthermore, he's one of the few men I've met who genuinely appreciates the importance of a woman's career."

"Her career!" He looked surprised, ignoring the fact that it was his turn to play. "What's that got to do with anything?"

Reva laughed with wry comprehension. "You're like so many other men, Josh, with no understanding of the value of a woman's career to herself and to the marriage. But to me it's crucial and I need a man who fully accepts that. Are you going to play or not?"

He hesitated, the dark brows drawing together as he considered her words. Then he finally selected a card, adding it to his hand with seeming disinterest. It was clear he was thinking of their conversation instead.

"You have no intention of subordinating your career to your husband's?" he demanded after a thoughtful moment.

"No," she said very firmly. "I was tempted once and it ended in disaster."

"What happened?" he pressed, watching as she studied her hand.

"Josh, a very long time ago a very wise woman tried to teach me something very important. . . ."

"What woman?" he demanded, the line of his brows growing darker.

"My mother. She found herself the sole support of herself and me after Dad divorced her, leaving almost no financial cushion. She went back to work after too many years out of the work force. Things were tough for a long time, to say the least. But with a lot of scrimping and saving and hard work she got me through college. The one thing she impressed upon me was that I must never allow myself to become economically dependent on a man. I must have a career of my own and be self-sufficient. I got through college with a degree in business administration and a solid background in computer science. My first job was a fabulous one with good money, great potential, and a lot of challenge. I loved it." Reva paused, thinking back. "But I thought I loved a man named Hugh Tyson even more."

"And he asked you to give up your job?" Josh interjected quietly, the card game now completely forgotten.

"We worked for the same company," Reva sighed, shaking her head. "He felt it would be impossible for us to maintain a serious romance without a lot of gossip which could damage his career." She took a deep breath, meeting the lion eyes across the teak table. "The long and the short of it is I agreed to leave the firm. After all, we were going to be married and it was obvious one of us had to quit. And since he was on a much higher managerial level than I was, it made economic sense for me to be the one to leave. I could always get another job somewhere else." Her mouth twisted wryly.

"Did you marry him?" Josh asked deliberately in a steady, almost gentle voice.

"No," Reva answered shortly. "Two weeks after I'd quit I found out he was having an affair with his secretary. Needless to say I was no longer interested in marriage. But I found myself out of a job and that turned into a major problem. It took me a year to find something anywhere near as good as the position I had left. As it was I had to take a cut in salary and wait longer for the first promotion. In effect, quitting set me back almost two full years. I was twenty-five at the time and I've worked very hard since then to reestablish my career. I learned my lesson, to put it mildly."

"So that's why you haven't married," he noted softly. "You've been rebuilding a career and making certain you didn't get burned again."

"Exactly. I suppose it's become a kind of obsession with me. But there's more to it than just a basic desire not to be economically dependent on a man who might casually walk out at any time. During the process of rebuilding my career my job has come to mean a great deal to me. I like working. It's become an intrinsic part of my life and one which I wouldn't give up even if I suddenly inherited a lot of money and could afford to quit forever. I like the power of being in management and I enjoy the challenge. There's a satisfaction to be had in my work which I couldn't get in any other way and I know that now. Perhaps the mistake I made when I was twenty-five made me appreciate all the more what I built afterward. I don't know. The one thing I am sure of is that when I finally do marry it's going to be to someone like Bruce who understands me." She put down her winning hand with a sudden flourish and grinned to shake off the heaviness of the atmosphere. "Gin!"

"And I cheated so hard," Josh complained, collapsing back into the pillows in self-disgust.

The rest of the day passed in quiet pursuits geared to the sickbed and Reva took a strange pleasure in soothing Josh's discomfort and tending to his small needs. He was a very undemanding patient, which made her all the more anxious to comfort him. She had the impression he was suffering more than he wanted to admit and she found his brave front touching.

"I really appreciate this, Reva," he told her in a heart-felt voice as she delivered the third cup of honey-and-lemon tea of the day. "Damn! but I feel like a fool imposing on you like this!"

"I don't mind, Josh," she assured him earnestly. "In a way it gives me a chance to repay you for the way you took care of me back in that jungle. Of course fixing you honey and lemon is hardly equivalent to saving your life, but it's something!" she added with a small laugh.

"The way I feel right now, it is more than equivalent to saving my life," he informed her with a grimace. "I'm hardly ever ill, but this thing really gets me down." He broke off at the sound of a knock on the door, sipping his tea as Reva went to answer it.

"Hello, Sandy, Tom," she smiled at the young couple from next door. "Come on in. I believe you already met my guest," she added with a grin as Sandy pushed her husband's wheelchair into the room. Tom Pierce had been confined to the chair for two months and he had another month to go before he would be free of it. Reva knew he was chafing at the trapped feeling and Sandy had more than once dropped in during the evenings to share a cup of coffee with her neighbor and recuperate from the strain of being at her husband's beck and call. She was very much in love with her good-looking, dark-headed husband but, as she had confessed to Reva, there were times when she could cheerfully have locked him in the closet for the sake of some peace and quiet.

"Good grief!" Sandy commented, seeing Josh tucked into a quilt on the couch. "Don't tell me we have another invalid on our hands!" She tossed her auburn curls and her green eyes sparkled at Reva with feminine laughter.

"I know you must have been glad to see him, Reva," Tom put in, shaking his head admonishingly, "but did you have to reduce your future husband to that state?"

Reva turned a brilliant shade of red and unwillingly met Josh's teasing gaze. "First things first," she announced grimly, planting her hands on her hips and facing the new arrivals. "I would like to straighten out your, uh, impression of this relationship. Josh Corbett is a friend of mine. But that's as far as it goes. I'm afraid he was reduced to implying there was more to it than that because he was trying to find me last night and figured people would be inclined to help in the process if they thought they were aiding some secret romance. That's it!" She waited challengingly for any comments.

"A friend?" Sandy repeated delicately, tilting her pretty

head to one side as she took a seat in the Chinese garden print chair across from the couch.

"A friend," Josh assured her, smiling blandly.

"Remember that mess I wound up in on my vacation a few months ago?" Reva said, heading toward the kitchen to make coffee for her guests. "I told you about it one night when you were over here visiting."

"I remember," Tom said immediately, his curious dark eyes on Josh.

"Well, this is the man who got me out of it," Reva said calmly. Sandy and Tom were about the only ones to whom she had told the story and that was only because she had been going through a particularly bad bout of nightmares. She had thought it might help to talk to someone, and her neighbors had proven sympathetic listeners. Nevertheless, she hadn't told them everything, and she now let Josh know that by sending him a silent signal as she crossed the carpet with a tray. He met her eyes and she knew he'd gotten the message.

"No kidding?" Tom said with an enthusiastic note in his voice. Sandy glanced interestedly at her husband and Reva knew the look was prompted by the fact that Tom hadn't been enthusiastic about much of anything lately. "I'd like to hear the whole story sometime, Josh. Reva gave us a brief outline but she didn't have the full picture of what was happening around her, I gather. The papers carried only a couple of small headlines and then dropped the tale. Revolutionary coups seem to be a dime a dozen in that part of the world. How did you happen to be down there at the time?" Tom accepted his cup of coffee from Reva, his eyes on the older man.

"I was there on business," Josh began slowly, and went on to give the political details of the situation to a fascinated Tom. The conversation lasted for a good portion of the afternoon, sparked by a continuing series of intelligent questions from Reva's next-door neighbor. Fortunately, Josh glossed briefly over the three days he'd spent with Reva, smiling across the room at her as he did so. There was an intimate, teasing aspect in the curve of his mouth which invited her to note how diplomatic he was being on the subject.

It was Reva who finally brought the discussion to a halt, frowning a little worriedly as Josh clearly began to tire. She made a quiet remark about her patient getting some rest and Sandy nodded at once. It was an effort getting Tom to agree to leave, but his wife handled the problem by taking a firm hold on the wheelchair and propelling him out the door.

"Just wait until I'm back on my feet, woman," Tom grumbled good-naturedly as he was whisked away. "I'm going to remember all this high-handed treatment!"

"Promises, promises," Sandy teased, waving good-bye to Reva and shutting the door behind them.

"How are you feeling, Josh?" Reva asked solicitously as she cleared away the cups and saucers. "Perhaps you should take a nap? I'm going to have to run out to the store for something for dinner, I'm afraid. I don't generally keep much on hand."

"So you won't be tempted to munch?" he chuckled, lounging back under the quilt with a sigh.

"Yes, but since you're here . . ."

"I get the impression I'm about to be used as an excuse so that you can treat yourself to a decent meal," he remarked, watching her move about.

"Perhaps you aren't very hungry, what with not feeling well and all. . . ." she said at once with a serious expression.

"I'll be starving by dinnertime," he assured her.

"Oh, good! Do you like ravioli?" she asked hopefully.

"With heaps and heaps of Parmesan cheese," he murmured encouragingly.

"Lovely!" Reva spent a charmed moment thinking of the delights ahead of her and then brought herself back to the present. "I'd better be on my way, then," she said briskly, heading for the coat closet. "I'll get some more fruit juice for you, too."

"And perhaps some ice cream for my sore throat?" he suggested helpfully.

"Chocolate or vanilla?" she demanded, her hand on the doorknob.

"Your choice," he told her magnanimously.

Several hours later, replete from a sinfully good meal of ravioli, salad, crusty bread, and chocolate sundaes, Reva poured the last drops of the Chianti wine she had bought to go with dinner and moved her playing piece on the checker board with a gleeful air.

"And down you go to ringing defeat once again," she announced grandly as Josh surrendered with a groan.

"Don't you feel a little mean taking advantage of a sick man this way?"

"Not when you're so much bigger than I am."

"What's size got to do with skill?" he retorted, collecting checkers and piling them back into the box.

"Nothing, it would appear," Reva smiled innocently. "You haven't won a single game we've played all evening. Cards, checkers, Chinese marbles . . ."

"I've explained that I'm ill," he defended himself.

"Excuses, excuses. How about television? Can you manage that?" she inquired, pulling out the weekly TV supplement from the newspaper and leaning back beside him on the couch to study it intently.

"Depends," he hedged, glancing over her shoulder. "Any good movies?"

"Well, let's see. There's a Western," she said with relish.

"Nope."

"There's a horror flick. . . ." She cocked an eye up at him to see if he was interested.

"Nope. Keep going."

"Here's a mystery." She mentioned it in a deliberately neutral tone, not wanting to influence him.

"What sort of mystery?" he asked at once.

"One of those elegant British things where some little old ladies go around doing in various gentlemen."

"Terrific," he said enthusiastically. "Let's watch that. Unless you'd rather see something else?" he added quickly, politely.

"Oh, no," she smiled, getting up to turn on the set. "This is my kind of film. I love these sophisticated old thrillers."

"Me, too," he grinned as she came back to join him on the couch.

They spent the next two and a half hours cheering for the little old ladies and trading odd bits of trivia on British mystery authors in general, but when the last commercial was over, Reva got to her feet with determination.

"Bedtime for you," she told her patient firmly. "I should never have let you stay up to see that film. You're probably exhausted. Up you go. You can brush your teeth while I'm making the couch back into a bed." She frowned worriedly as he obediently wrapped the quilt around himself and stood up. "Can you make it all right? Still feeling dizzy when you stand?"

"A little wobbly, but I'll take it slow. I'll help you with the couch."

"No, that's all right," she told him, puttering around and getting things organized in her usual efficient matter. "Just be careful on the way to the bath!"

"Yes, ma'am," he murmured in such a low voice she almost didn't hear him. When she shot him a fierce look he smiled, abashed. "Sorry. I'm not used to being fussed over."

She relented with a small grin. "Life is full of new experiences."

It wasn't the nightmare which woke Reva some time later, but an unfamiliar sound from the living room. Her eyes flickered open sleepily and she met the equally sleepy gaze of Xavier, who was curled in the middle of her covers, his head resting on her foot. He blinked his green eyes once, as if to tell her he'd heard the noise, too, and then went back to sleep. From which, Reva told herself, she could deduce that nothing terrible was amiss.

Still, she decided, eyeing the ceiling thoughtfully, the noise was undoubtedly caused by Josh, who might be having trouble sleeping. Or perhaps he'd gotten up for a drink of water and suffered another dizzy spell. She frowned to herself and then threw off the covers, reaching for her robe.

Tiptoeing was hardly necessary on the luxurious carpet, but Reva moved carefully nonetheless as she made her way out into the living room. In the pale city glow streaming in from the huge picture windows she saw Josh's large figure sprawled across the bed, the covers hanging over the edge where he'd apparently tossed them in a fit of restlessness. She went forward worriedly, wondering if he was suffering from another bout of fever. He had seemed to be getting better during the day but perhaps the evening activities had been too much for him.

He was wearing only a pair of shorts and she had the

impression that that much clothing at night was only being worn out of deference to her. The fact that she had once seen him in less had not been mentioned by either of them all day. She reached the edge of the bed, her eyes running gently over his lean, tanned body. With a strangely maternal feeling she began to rearrange the covers back over him. She knew, deep inside, that in spite of the fact that he wasn't really a mercenary, this man had led a rather hard life. She thought about all the times he'd had to nurse himself through this strange malady he'd contracted and shook her head a little sadly. Like Xavier, Josh Corbett could take care of himself, but there was something about both males that reached out to her. Something that made her want to provide a bit of softness in their lives.

With a slight shake of her head Reva told herself not to be fanciful and settled the last of the covers back over the patient. As she did so, Josh turned fretfully in his sleep. Was he feverish? Was that why he'd pushed them aside in the first place? Josh twisted again and Reva leaned down to put her hand gently on his forehead. Instantly he seemed to relax. He didn't seem too warm, she thought, sitting carefully down beside him and letting her hand stroke his head lightly. With a small sound Josh turned his face into her robe-clad thigh and seemed to sink at once into a deeper, more restful slumber.

Reva sat there a long time, afraid to move for fear of bringing back the restlessness in him. She kept her fingers on him, moving them in light, soothing motions across his forehead and into the silver at his temples. As he slept quietly she watched the gleam of late-night city lights through her window and wondered what Josh Corbett would do when he was well enough to leave her apartment. The man didn't seem to have any real home. He'd told her he had an apartment in Houston where his energy-oriented company was based, but from his brief description of it earlier in the day it sounded more like a motel room he used when he happened to be in that part of the country. It was almost an hour before Reva crept softly back to her own bed leaving Josh sleeping peacefully behind her.

The next morning Reva made no mention to Josh of his restlessness during the night and he appeared to have no recollection of it, for which she was grateful. She couldn't fully explain to herself her feelings as she'd sat by his bed, and had no desire to try and explain her actions to him!

"Eggs Benedict!" he exclaimed happily when she'd set a breakfast tray on the teak coffee table and taken a seat opposite him. "Still using me as an excuse to eat properly?"

"It doesn't take much of an excuse for me," she retorted tartly, pouring orange juice. "Having a guest in the house is as good a reason as any other!"

"Does Tanner know about your secret dieting?" Josh asked comfortably, taking up his fork with relish.

"We've never discussed it. I can't see that it matters particularly!"

"It seems to me that he deserves to know. If you marry him one of two things is going to happen. Either you put him on your own regime or else you use him as an excuse to splurge. Either way he's going to be in for a shock. One way he'll find himself starving all week and the other he'll watch you putting on weight. My advice is to come clean with him, Reva," Josh concluded knowledgeably. "Who knows? Maybe he'll like you with a little more weight on your bones!"

"Thank you for your concern," Reva snapped crisply,

plunging into her high-calorie egg dish. "I'll worry about it when the time comes. Speaking of Bruce, what are you going to do while I'm out with him this evening? Will you be all right by yourself or do you want me to arrange to have Sandy and Tom look in on you?"

"I can take care of myself," he retorted briefly. "I've done it before."

"Yes, I know, but . . ."

"I'll entertain myself with your collection of Mozart and mysteries," he smiled suddenly.

She frowned and then relaxed. "Oh, you've been checking out the contents of my bookcase, have you?"

"And your record cabinet. I peeked while you were making breakfast."

"You must be feeling better?"

"Umm," he agreed noncommittally. "By tomorrow I should be completely back on my feet, or at least clearly on the mend. And tonight I'll be quite content with your books and your records."

"You like Mozart?" she asked in slow surprise.

"And Haydn and Bach. All of which you seemed to have in abundance," he nodded, pleased.

"The concert tonight is going to be composed mostly of Mozart concertos," Reva said on a little burst of enthusiasm.

"I'm sorry I'll miss it. But I'll put some on here and think of you while I read that new mystery I see you've got checked out from the library. Being out of touch for four months, I didn't know that author had done another one recently."

Reva nodded and started to comment on it when she thought of something. "Josh, you won't wait up for me, will you? You need your sleep."

"Don't worry, I'll be sound asleep long before you get in. Although," he added mildly, slanting a curious lion glance at her, "I don't imagine you'll be all that late, will you? You have to go to work in the morning."

"No, I won't be late."

Things were a bit awkward when Bruce arrived at seven o'clock that evening. Josh was firmly established amid a pile of quilts on the couch, Xavier on his lap. A Mozart record was already on the stereo and he was well into chapter one of the mystery novel. He looked up with a smile which Reva privately considered a little too gracious when she emerged from the bedroom to open the door. The sophisticated, long-sleeved dress of blue-green jersey matched her eyes and it swirled gracefully around her ankles as she greeted her escort for the evening. Her hair was folded into a soft, flattering curve anchored at the top of her head, and long, sparkling earrings accented the line of her throat.

Josh was all charm and geniality, ignoring the stiffness of Bruce's greeting and advising the younger man to have a pleasant evening with Reva. There was a certain annoying attitude of familiarity about Josh's manner as he bade the other two good-night, but Reva couldn't quite put her finger on any one thing to criticize and decided it was probably her imagination.

As soon as they were out the door, she had to spend a considerable amount of time soothing Bruce's suspicious questions, which got the evening off to a rather bad beginning. Things improved a bit at the concert as Reva did her best to set her escort's unhappiness over Josh's presence at ease. Over and over again she explained the illness and for the first time gave Bruce a very sketchy description of why she was indebted to Corbett.

"I understand your thinking," Bruce said finally, shortly before he said good night to her in front of her door. "But I still think the man is imposing on you. Gratitude only requires so much from you, Reva," he added with a lecturing frown.

"I know, Bruce, but he'll be gone soon. He's much better today and I fully expect him to be on his way in a day or two," she assured him. "I'd invite you in for a nightcap," she went on hesitantly, "but he'll be asleep. . . . Next time?"

Bruce sighed. "I'll look forward to it," he said politely and then, much to Reva's surprise, he took her somewhat aggressively into his arms. Bruce was usually not the aggressive sort. His mild lovemaking on their past few dates had been limited to some agreeable but definitely not aggressive kisses. Nevertheless, she endured it politely, searching herself for some sign of genuine response. This was the man she was seriously considering marrying. Why was there none of the beguiling temptation she had experienced in Josh's arms? But sex, she reminded herself grimly, wasn't everything.

Several minutes later she watched as a slightly more satisfied Bruce stepped into the elevator and waved a last good-bye. Then she opened her door and crept silently past a sleeping Josh. There was no movement from him as she made her way to her room and only Xavier greeted her in a sleepy, catlike way.

But she found her bed turned back and a flower from the arrangement on the dining-room table was lying on her pillow. Reva found herself smiling a small, secret little smile as she slipped into bed.

But the feminine pleasure with which she'd climbed

into bed wasn't sufficient defense against the recurring nightmare. Once more it brought Reva out of a sound sleep with a pounding heart and a vague, undefined feeling of fear. This time her first instinctive reaction was that safety was at hand. It was as close as the next room where Josh lay sound asleep.

CHAPTER FIVE

Trembling with reaction to the generalized fear in the dream, Reva got slowly out of bed. She had herself under control, she thought grimly. After all, she had dealt with this thing in the past. It was just that she knew the sight of Josh would bring her back to normal faster than the warm glass of milk or turning on the television, remedies she had used at various times since she'd returned from South America.

She would go quietly into the living room, take a few deep breaths, and assure her subconscious mind that Josh, large and protective, was nearby. Apparently she hadn't cried out this time because there was no sign of movement from the couch bed as she went shakily into the living room. Either she hadn't called his name this time or else Josh was too sound asleep to have heard her.

Clutching her robe tightly around her waist, Reva stood at the foot of the unfolded couch and stared at the strange man from her past as he lay sleeping in the pale darkness. Tonight he seemed less restless, one part of her mind noted. He hadn't kicked off the covers as he had the previous night.

She stood silently, taking the deep breaths she'd promised herself and finding the sight of his dark head against the pillow as calming as she had known instinctively it

91

would be. Gradually the incipient terror receded from her limbs, leaving her feeling weak and curiously vulnerable. She knew she was longing now for more than the sight of Josh. She wanted to know the heat of his body and the sense of protection she had experienced before in his arms. How could she deny it?

He was all wrong for her, she knew that. He was hard and capable of violence. She was certain that the civilizing veneer was as thin on him as it was on Xavier. But during the past couple of days she had seen a side of him she wouldn't have suspected existed. It wasn't a weak or soft side, in spite of his illness. It was more that, like her cat, Josh was capable of taking pleasure in the gentler side of life when it was available. The comparison made Reva smile and almost unconsciously she stepped a little closer, rounding the foot of the bed to stand beside him.

She couldn't seem to take her eyes off him tonight now that she was so close. She should never have left the bedroom to seek his presence, regardless of the calming effect it was having on her nerves. But even as she told herself that, Reva found herself sitting carefully down beside him as she had done last night, putting out a hand to touch his forehead. She told herself she was only testing for signs of fever, but she didn't remove her hand when she found none.

Only a few more minutes, Reva promised herself, that's all she would allow. Then she would go back to her own room. If he stirred or woke how would she ever explain herself? But he did neither. He made no threatening or alarming moves at all and Reva found herself wanting to edge closer. The fear caused by her nightmare was almost completely dissipated. There was nothing holding her close to Josh except her desire to be there. With a small, accepting sigh, Reva admitted as much to herself.

Soon this man would be gone once more from her life, she thought with a strange pang. And it would be all for the best. He was completely wrong for her. His career lay thousands of miles away in Texas and even if that weren't a factor, she needed someone like Bruce who was sophisticated and sympathetic to her goals and ambitions. Reva had no doubt at all that if Josh had truly wanted to marry her he would have expected her to give up everything for him. He was that sort of man. Possessive and ultimately always in command. It was ingrained in his nature. Then she thought of how he liked Mozart and mysteries and once again she smiled a little. A strange mixture in a male. But there were a lot of enigmatic factors in Josh Corbett. Not least of which was this pull he had on her senses.

A pull that tonight, at least, she no longer wanted to deny. With a sharply indrawn breath at her own daring and a last nod to common sense, Reva gently tugged back the quilt and slipped into bed beside Josh.

There was still no movement from Josh's lean, silent body as Reva's toe came into contact with his leg. He was lying sprawled on his stomach, his head turned away from her and his arms flung outward. Hesitantly, not wanting to admit but unable to deny the pleasure it gave her, Reva put her hand on his back and stroked lightly down to his waist. Her fingers trailed over the contours of his muscles and down to the lean hardness of the edge of his hip. Memories of how she had lost herself in his embrace that last night in the jungle and how she had almost begged for his love on his first night in her apartment returned with a sensual rush, blotting out the last remnants of rational thinking. Every instinct in her body wanted to suspend the reasoning side of her nature tonight and allow the senses to assume full control.

Once again she stroked her fingertips across his shoulders, hardly touching the bare, tanned skin. It wasn't too late, a small voice advised in her head, Josh hadn't awakened. She could slip back out of his bed and return to her own, leaving him none the wiser and herself with nothing to explain in the morning. It was undoubtedly what she should do, she thought, trying to give some attention to the voice of common sense. And there was still time.

Halfheartedly but nevertheless with deliberate intent, Reva removed her hand from Josh's back and pulled her toe away from where it touched his leg. She would only live to regret it if she stayed here tonight, she told herself.

But even as she gently slid her foot back toward the edge of the bed the decision was taken out of her hands. With a compellingly purposeful movement, Josh's leg snaked out and found her retreating ankle.

Reva gave a small, surprised gasp as she felt him anchor her foot firmly to the bed. Had it been an accidental move in his sleep? She continued to try edging away but his broad shoulders rose, blocking out her view of distant city lights, and then he was leaning over her, his arms somehow trapping her as he put his hands on either side of her body. She couldn't read his expression.

"Josh?" she whispered, staring wide eyed up into his face. The golden lion gaze blazed down at her but there was no answer. Instead, he bent his head to take her lips in a devastating kiss that seemed composed of equal parts of savagery and tenderness. A kiss that contained the essence of the man, Reva thought distantly even as she succumbed to its impact.

Any last thoughts of trying to make it safely back to her own bed disappeared completely as the basic, feminine core of Reva accepted the fact that this time there was no escape. Josh's large, powerful body settled heavily across hers, holding her in a sensual, erotic cage that permitted no possibility of retreat.

"My God! You weigh a ton!" Reva whispered breathlessly. "I'd forgotten. How could I have forgotten?" Her arms wound around his neck, seeking to know the full heaviness of him. For some reason his sheer weight and strength were a powerful summons to her responses. It was as if her body craved the overwhelming virility of him above all the other pleasures of the world.

With small, husky moans, Reva returned the passionate embrace, parting her lips when his tongue demanded entrance, arching her soft breasts against his chest, trembling with each new touch of his possessive, probing fingers.

Still he said nothing and Reva heard herself uttering the few coherent words that were spoken, telling him of her need, of her joy in him, and of her desires. When he shifted his body momentarily, she thought he was abandoning the embrace and cried out in protest but a few seconds later she felt his hard, tantalizing fingers find the opening of her robe, pushing it off her shoulders. Her nightgown soon followed and she lay fully nude beneath him. With hands that shook with desire Reva managed to strip the one garment he wore from his body.

With no barrier between them Josh once again closed the embrace until Reva was aware of him on every square inch of her body. She felt the hardness of his manhood and shivered in response. His mouth moved heatedly, moistly on hers and then sought out the delicate, vulnerable areas of her throat.

"Oh, yes, Josh," she gasped as the hair of his chest scraped roughly across her nipples, creating tiny tremors that soon hardened the tips of her breasts into two crests of desire. His strong fingers moved to reinforce the sensation, playing first gently and then with increasing urgency over her breasts until they settled at the sensitive nipples and concentrated on generating a fiery, clamoring need.

"Touch me, hold me, love me," Reva moaned over and over again, curving herself into the warmth of his thighs. Her hands kneaded the muscles of his shoulders and then her nails trailed down his back, seeking the base of his spine and the masculine hips beyond. Although he still said nothing, there was a vibrant, hoarsely male groan of response as she deepened her intimate exploration of his body. She heard his breathing thicken and increase in pace as did her own.

His hand caught her twisting, churning lower body, his fingers digging almost fiercely into the soft skin of her hip and then he was sliding slowly, erotically down the length of her, dropping deep, passionate kisses at every point along the way. The small bones at the hollow of her shoulder, the tip of her breast, her navel, and the small mound below her stomach. Reva thought she would go crazy with the growing force of her own desire. She prodded the base of his neck, delighting in the smooth band of musculature she encountered, and then, as he teased the region of her stomach with his kisses and his tongue, she slid her fingers up to clench furiously in the thickness of his hair.

"Ah!" The cry was torn from her as Josh first kissed and then gently bit the soft, inner part of her thigh. In a silent fury of rising passion he rained more of the gentle, stinging kisses over her body, his hands alternately squeezing and caressing her legs down their length until he encountered her ankle, and then his fingers worked back up her body. The rest of him followed, rolling slowly over the surface of her like a giant tidal wave that caught everything in its path and whirled it up into the mounting crest.

As his ravaging, aggressive mouth once again approached her lips, pausing to drop further urgent kisses at waist and shoulder, Reva felt her passion intensify until she thought she couldn't take any more of the explosive, erotic buildup. Already she was gasping for air and pleading for the ultimate embrace. Her body curved beseechingly up into his rocklike weight. And then, at long last, he spoke.

"Reva!" Her name in a husky, demanding, possessive growl uttered at the same moment that he completed the union in a surge of power. Power that sent shock waves radiating out to the tips of Reva's fingers and the soles of her arching feet. She couldn't even cry out.

Her name came hoarsely from between his lips again and again as the pace of his lovemaking accelerated into a tension-bound pattern that led Reva toward a peak of experience she had had never known before Josh and had not known since that night in the jungle four months ago. It was beyond anything she could possibly have described. There were no words for the endless moment in time. So Reva clung with all her might to the strength and power and elemental maleness of the man who held her in bonds of primitive passion. And when, together, they rode the wave Josh had set in motion to its culmination, they were both washed up on the sand to be left in a tangle of damp, spent bodies.

For a long time Reva refused to think of anything at all, lying quietly under the weight of Josh's outflung arm and leg and listening to his labored breathing return to normal. But the moment out of time couldn't last forever and a part of her knew it. Sooner or later Reva realized she was going to have to face the reality of what she had just done. It was Josh who broke the spell. Levering himself up slowly on one elbow, he looked at her in the shadowy light, the possessive satisfaction in his eyes a palpable wave of heat as he drank in the sight of her.

Reva stared back at him, her wide, questioning eyes reflecting her inner thoughts as the full impact of the situation hit her. What had she done? What had she *done*?

"Does this mean," Josh inquired with the wicked humor of a man who knows he's just had his victory handed to him on a platter, "that I no longer have to play sick?" He put out an arrogant hand to rest warmly on her bare stomach, clearly enjoying the feel of her.

It was not the lead-in statement Reva had expected to the conversation she knew must come, and she blinked her sea-colored eyes as she struggled through its meaning. Surely he hadn't tricked her! She couldn't have been that stupid.

"What are you talking about, Josh?" she said very carefully, trying to adjust herself to the odd direction of the discussion. She must have misunderstood!

"I mean that, as much fun as it is lounging around your apartment all day and having you wait on me hand and foot, I think it would be even more amusing if I could revert to my normal, disgustingly healthy self. Not that I haven't enjoyed the cosseting, you understand. It's a rare experience for me and I shall treasure it, but . . ."

"Josh!" she interrupted with gathering fury, but still managing to keep her temper within bounds, "Have you been lying to me this weekend? You weren't really sick?" She wanted to make very certain of his guilt before unleashing the full force of her abused feelings, she told herself righteously.

"Not exactly, sweetheart," he murmured, the fingers on her stomach tracing an idle little pattern. "Let's just say I was a little sick to find out I wasn't going to get the hero's welcome I had been expecting."

Reva struggled to a sitting position, the beginnings of an infuriated glare drawing her fine features into a tight mask. Her eyes deepened their sea shade until they became angry pools in the dim room. Her anger was as much at herself as it was at the man watching her intently, but, being larger, he made the better target, she decided.

"Hero's welcome!" she bit out tightly. "What on earth gave you the idea you deserved such a welcome? I don't normally go around thanking men who do me favors by letting them into my bed!" She became suddenly aware of her own nudity and snatched up the sheet, holding it to her throat with one hand while she braced herself against the back of the couch with the other. Her hair spilled around her shoulders in a tousled disarray and her eyes blazed.

"I guess I wanted to be the exception," Josh grinned unrepentantly. He was eyeing her intently, but the hint of wariness she'd seen in his expression from time to time during the weekend was gone. Josh thought himself home at last, she realized bleakly. And that catlike satisfaction was as difficult to fight in him as it had been when she had first seen it in Xavier the night she had relented and given him the first saucer of milk.

"Then consider yourself rewarded," she hissed spitefully, her chaotic emotions making it difficult to even think straight. What was she going to do now? "You can pack your bag and get out of here," she added vengefully, "because there won't be any follow-up rewards. I can guarantee that! I've been a fool for the past couple of days to be taken in by your little act and I was an even bigger fool tonight, but fortunately that sort of stupidity is curable. Damn you, Josh! How could you do this to me? You said you liked me. . . . You claimed you wanted to marry me! How could any man who felt anything meaningful for a woman trick her and lie to her?" Her voice was threatening to crack, Reva thought, horrified. She mustn't lose her self-control. It would be the ultimate humiliation. She edged farther away from him, dragging the sheet with her. Her eyes were suspiciously damp as she watched him in mingled reproach and fury.

"Calm down, honey," he smiled soothingly, making no move to stop her from sliding to the edge of the bed. "There's nothing to be upset about and you know it. I had to do something to stop you from kicking me out of your apartment and getting conveniently ill was the only thing that came to mind on the spur of the moment. It gave you a chance to relax and get to know me again, didn't it? For some reason you'd spent the last four months building up a mental barrier against me. You looked absolutely shocked when I found you in that restaurant the other night." He shook his head slightly, as if finding her fears on a par with those of a child.

"On the contrary," Reva snapped, "I find it extremely upsetting to know what a fool I've made of myself. I can't believe I've gotten myself into such a mess," she groaned, twisting to sit up shakily on the edge of the bed, the sheet wrapped around her. Unable to meet his eyes now she stared fixedly across the room at the Chinese screen that decorated the far wall. "It's that crazy nightmare," she whispered, half to herself. "If it hadn't been for that . . ."

"You would have still been sleeping peacefully in your own bed and I would have still been sick in the morning," Josh finished gently, as he sat up behind her. With astonishingly sensitive fingers he stroked the line of her spine beneath the partial covering of the sheet and Reva shivered in response. "Now, thanks to your instincts which told you to come looking for me when you're afraid, everything's out in the open. We can both go on from here. Stop fighting yourself, Reva. You're only wasting time. You belong to me and I'm going to keep you with me. It's all very simple, really."

"Simple!" She could have wept with bitterness and frustration. "What's simple about it? I keep telling you, Josh, that there's no basis for any kind of lasting relationship between us. We're different, so different. . . ."

"I suppose we are in some ways," he surprised her by admitting in a musing tone. His fingers continued to massage her spine as he talked. "I'm all the things you said I was: hard and ill-mannered at times and perhaps overly aggressive when I'm going after something I want . . ."

"That's putting it mildly!"

"And you're softer, more civilized and sophisticated," he went on, ignoring her. "You like the finer things in life and you're accustomed to men who will leave you at your front door with a good-night kiss even though they know there's another man waiting inside."

"You listened! You were awake when Bruce said good night to me out there in the corridor?" she accused furiously, swiveling around to face him.

"How could I sleep knowing you were out with another man, even if I was certain you'd be coming home to me?" He shrugged blandly. "Naturally I was awake and I know he simply kissed you good-night and went on his way. Not that I intend to allow even that much in the future," he added with a promising little smile. "But tonight you were lucky. I decided to tolerate it. If he's such a fool as to let you keep me under the same roof, he's really not worth worrying about."

"Bruce is a very understanding person," Reva defended

her escort. "I wouldn't expect you to comprehend what that means, of course, but . . ."

"It means he's either not very bright or he's gotten a little too sophisticated and soft. Perhaps he's just too young," Josh declared dismissingly. "In any event, it doesn't matter. He's obviously not going to put up much of a fight so I can't get overly concerned. Besides, that's all behind us, Reva."

"Why didn't you say something when I came in this evening if you were awake?" she gritted, thinking of this man calmly waiting up for her to make sure she came home to him and then turning over and going to sleep. It was enough to annoy any woman, but she wasn't exactly certain why. Surely she hadn't wanted him to make a scene! She hated scenes!

There was a slight pause as if Josh was not certain whether or not to reply, and then he said neutrally, "The truth is, even though I don't really see your Bruce as a threat, I didn't find the notion of you spending the evening with him particularly good on the nerves or the temper. I didn't want an argument with you that would put you even more on the defensive, so I decided it was best to keep quiet and let you tiptoe off to bed. How was I to know you would take matters into your own two lovely hands and put everything right before the evening was over?"

"Making a fool out of myself doesn't put things right, Josh. It only complicates them terribly. Why can't you see that? You'll have to leave."

. "I have no intention of leaving. An intelligent man doesn't walk out when he's finally retrieved his treasure," he told her tersely. "But why do you keep saying that? You don't really want me to leave and you know it. You can't make love to a man the way you just made love to me and then decide you've changed your mind again!"

"Why not?" she whispered bleakly, scanning the crinkling lines at the corners of his eyes and wondering how she was ever going to get herself and her life back to normal. She could not be in love with this man. That's all there was to it. She would not allow it!

"Reva," he told her with the first touch of harsh impatience in the deep, rough voice, "don't try and convince me you're thinking in terms of a one-night stand. I know you too well."

"You still think you want marriage?" she husked, looking away from him.

"It's the only answer for us, Reva. I want a home and you and that means marriage. I've rattled around alone long enough and I'm tired of it. I want a home of my own with a warm and vital woman who will fit me into her life-style even though I'm a little alien to it. I want slippers and a hearth and a huge chair in which I can lounge in the evenings with you on my lap and Xavier at my feet. I don't want to be left out in the cold any longer with only an occasional fleeting encounter to warm my nights. Is that so hard to understand? Perhaps if I'd had all that when I was younger I wouldn't appreciate it or long for it like I do. I know other men my age who go crazy and leave it all behind chasing some brief adventure. But I've had my fill of the adventuring, both physical and emotional. When I found you in that jungle in South America everything crystallized for me. I knew you were my ticket to everything I'd missed."

"A fixation," Reva said dully. "It's as I said that first night you came back. You've developed some sort of fixation on me."

"Call it whatever you want," he grated softly. "But you've developed the same for me!"

"No!"

"Then why haven't you told Tanner about the nightmares?" he snapped back instantly. "Why haven't you invited him into your bed, used him to comfort yourself when you woke up afraid!"

"Stop it, Josh!" Reva begged, her voice ragged with a sense of despair.

"Not until I finally wring some of the truth out of you," he vowed, moving with a surprising swiftness to wrap one arm around her middle and haul her back into the bed. Startled and painfully angry, she lay beneath him as he anchored her into the bedclothes.

"Damn it! Take your hands off me!" she ordered, infuriated.

"You're mine, Reva," he growled, not releasing her. The honey-colored eyes were filled with pure determination and impatience. "I made you mine four months ago and you finally acknowledged it on some level at least when you came looking for me tonight."

"That's not true! It was the nightmare. . . ." she began desperately.

"And was it the nightmare that brought you out to my bedside last night?" he put in coolly, using his weight quite unmercifully to pin her. His hands framed her tortured face, his thumbs stroking the hair back at her temples. "I could have reached out and taken you then. Did you realize that, Reva? Instead I contented myself with the feel of you trying to soothe my fevered brow." He smiled abruptly. "I was afraid you'd realize I was getting well fairly quickly when you couldn't sense any sign of a temperature, but it was worth the risk to have you show me some compassion."

"I was worried about you," she explained a little sadly, thinking of her stupidity. "I honestly thought you were sick and you'd seemed restless."

"I *was* restless. I had a hell of a time sleeping knowing you were in the other room!" he chuckled with fond wryness. "But when you came out to check on me I was afraid to make any move which might frighten you off again, so I relaxed and let you pet me. And my patience paid off, didn't it, little one? Tonight you didn't come out here just to pet me. Tonight you came looking for what we'd had together in that hut."

"You don't understand," Reva wailed, knowing there were no more lines of defense. How could she begin to explain the fact that she'd crawled into his bed of her own free will? The nightmare tale only went so far as an excuse. And that's all it had been, she admitted to herself. An excuse.

"You don't understand yourself, honey," he told her, lion eyes gleaming. "But one of these days you will. In the meantime there's no point fighting me and your instincts. I'm like your cat. I've found a home and I've moved in. You'll never be rid of me, Reva." There was undisguised triumph in him and something very female in Reva reacted to it at once.

"Never, Josh?" she breathed. "What about when you go back to work in Houston?"

There was a second's blank astonishment in the eyes which glittered so close to her face and she knew a small but despairing sense of success.

"You'll come with me," he stated matter-of-factly. "You'll *have* to come with me."

"I won't, Josh," she whispered with growing certainty. "I once gave up my job for someone I thought loved me and it was a disaster. I'm not about to repeat that disaster for anyone. Especially not someone who's developed some sort of thing about hearth and home. A whim which could disappear overnight."

"You think I would ask you to give up your life here and come to Texas with me if I didn't intend to take care of you?" he demanded, sounding incensed.

"I think you mean well at the moment, Josh, but who's to say how you'll feel in a month or two?" He had developed some sort of obsession, constructed some sort of myth about what she represented in his life, Reva told herself over and over. He was not in love with her. Men like this didn't think in terms of love. They thought in terms of possession and desire. She must remember that always. He was much too hard and tough to know the meaning of love. And it wasn't as if she were in love with him, she added silently to herself. Josh Corbett was unique in her life and she could admit, with some shame, to a desire for him which had overwhelmed her this evening. But she could control that. She must.

"You don't trust me to look after you, Reva?" he asked disbelievingly. The palms framing her face seemed to tighten and she could feel a new tension in him. "Honey, I would never ask you to give up your life here if I wasn't fully committed to taking care of you. You must believe that!"

"Josh," she sighed bleakly. "There's so much more to it than that. Why is it so easy for a man to ask a woman to give up a career and follow him thousands of miles to a strange place where she'll have to start all over? Do you know what it's like rebuilding a career? It's fine to leave one job for a better position, but to walk out of something good and established and satisfying in the hopes of finding something equal to it is a very traumatic experience."

"I agree," he said gently. "And it should only be asked in a situation where the man knows his own mind thoroughly and realizes the woman he's asking to make the sacrifice is the one woman for him. I know some men probably make the request lightly, unthinkingly, but I'm not one of them. I must have you with me, Reva, and I'm fully prepared to help you absorb the shock of the change. I've got some influence in Houston. I'll be able to help you find another position."

"That's not the point!" she cried wretchedly. "I don't want to move! I want what I've built here. It's as simple as that. Tell me, Josh, Would you move to Portland for me? Would you give up your job in Houston for the unknowns up here?"

"Reva, that wouldn't make any sense. I respect the work you do here, but I've got a good, solid hunch my job pays more and if we're going to live on one salary it's only reasonable it should be the larger. Besides, how could I ask you to marry me if I didn't have a job?"

"You're not answering my question. Yes or no?" she said tightly.

There was a fractional, almost curious pause before he said in a very low tone, "Are you asking me to do that, Reva?"

"No!" she flung back at once, sensing moisture behind her eyes as she met his gaze. "No. I would never dream of asking a man to give up everything for me."

"Why not, Reva?" he said quietly, a tinge of remoteness in the set lines of his craggy face. She was very conscious of his weight pressing her deep into the bed and a fleeting, treacherous tendril of thought reminded her of what that weight had been like while they were making love.

"Because I know that it would be asking too much of any man," she answered in a colorless tone.

"Asking too much of him because you couldn't make the commitment it would entail? It would mean everything, Reva," he said with a new and rather strange intensity. "I understand that. I realize that some men may have

107

become blind to the responsibilities and the depth of the certainty involved, but don't include me in their number. I am as fully conscious of them as you are. And I would not ask you to come with me to Texas unless I was sure of myself and of what we have together."

"But I am not as sure of us as you are, Josh," Reva sighed wistfully. "We are so different. The risk would be too great. And I can promise you I would not be the perfect little wife while I hunted for another job in Houston," she added with a bitter smile. "I know myself too well after the last experience. I would be resentful and tense and very unhappy. You would soon realize the dream wife you've conjured up in your imagination was only an illusion and then where would I be? If we no longer even had the strength of your . . . your fixation to hold us together we'd have another full-scale disaster on our hands, or, at least, I would have another disaster on my hands," she corrected herself bitterly. "You, of course, would have your work to console you. I would have nothing. Again."

"You were right," Josh said distantly, thoughtfully. "You really did learn your lesson when you were twenty-five, didn't you?"

Reva said nothing, only nodded her head once in an agonized kind of way that told its own story.

"And you're still not prepared to admit what you feel for me, either," he went on slowly. "Even though you're willing to share my bed."

"It won't happen again," she swore, more to herself than to him. "In spite of the evidence, I do have some self-control!"

"But it will happen again as long as I'm around to tempt you," he half-smiled, his mouth quirking wryly. "And I

108

intend to stay around. So there you are." He shrugged massively.

"Don't act so damned smug!" she grated fiercely. "I may have been weak tonight, but I'll be on my guard now, won't I? I won't let myself be softened up by your lies as I was this weekend!"

"Reva, honey," he vowed with great calm, "I'm not going back to Texas without you. I'm going to stay right here in Portland, as close to you as I can manage, and I'm going to do my level best to tempt you into my bed as often as possible. I will also tempt you in every other way I can think of to take me into your heart and your home. You've got yourself another stray alley cat, sweetheart," he mocked, "and I warn you I'm every bit as cagey and shrewd as Xavier is when it comes to getting what I want. What makes you think you can resist me? You're too soft, too compassionate, and, deep down, you want me too much to send me to the devil where I belong."

Reva lay very still, staring openmouthed at the stranger who had reentered her world and decided to stay. How did you get rid of a stray cat who was bigger, stronger, and far tougher than you were? Especially when you had more than once willingly let yourself become trapped between his protective and possessive paws?

CHAPTER SIX

"Things were a hell of a lot simpler," Josh remarked after a long moment as Reva continued to stare helplessly up at him, "back there in that jungle. You didn't try to hide behind a lot of civilized, intellectual barriers."

"I'm not trying to hide behind anything," Reva snapped, finding her voice at last. "As soon as I got home I realized we were all wrong for each other!"

"Because you thought I was some sort of hired killer," he concluded. "I can understand how you would feel mixed emotions about someone like that regardless of what you'd had with him." He was a little too glib in his "understanding," Reva decided suddenly.

"It's not that cut and dried," Reva protested, still held unmoving under the pressure of his body. "The reasons I decided you and I don't belong together had to do with other things than what I thought was your job. And those other things are still part of you, Josh." She looked at him pleadingly, but even as she tried to argue her case she could sense the weakness in herself and she had the awful premonition that Josh sensed it also. "You can be very hard and cold and ruthless. I saw it in South America and I know that side of you hasn't vanished."

"But I was never that way with you, Reva," he interrupted with a strange, rough passion in his voice. "With

111

you that side of me *does* vanish. For God's sake, don't ever be afraid of me, Reva! Whatever else happens, promise me that you'll never go in fear of me. I couldn't abide that."

Reva shuddered very slightly at the new degree of demand in his words. Something near desperation flickered briefly in the lion eyes and then disappeared at once. But not before Reva felt all her defenses momentarily dissolve beneath the sudden urge to reassure and comfort him. He really wanted to pretend he could turn his back on that harsher side of his nature and have the other side of life for his own. For an instant Reva saw him as she had first seen Xavier when the cat had demanded entrance into her home. She couldn't ignore the urgency of the desire and determination that burned steadily in Josh's eyes. She could answer this one question for him, at least.

"I'm not afraid of you, Josh," she said softly, lifting a hand to lightly touch the gray wings at his temples. She couldn't suppress the tender, compassionate smile which curved her mouth even though she knew it was equivalent to giving Xavier that initial saucer of milk and a place to stay for the night. She was weak when it came to this particular sort of fundamental male appeal and she might as well admit it to herself.

Instantly the tension in him evaporated and before Reva quite realized what he intended, Josh lowered his head to kiss her almost lightly on the lips. The caress held none of the driving passion she had known earlier, only a kind of thankfulness and gratitude which she hadn't expected. Did her small reassurance mean so much to him then? she asked herself wonderingly.

He didn't raise his head again but nestled down beside her on the pillow, turning his face to bury it in the soft stuff of her hair. "Marry me, Reva," he ordered in a thick, muffled voice. "Come with me to Houston and let me take care of you."

"Oh, Josh," she murmured desperately, wanting to cry, "you haven't understood anything I've tried to tell you tonight. I can't give up everything for a will-o'-the-wisp whim which may disappear overnight!"

"Then ask me to give up everything and marry you," he told her with the attitude of a large cat pouncing on a small, defenseless mouse.

He didn't move, his face still nuzzling her hair, but Reva jerked as if she'd been stung.

"What?" she gasped, astonished. Deliberately she struggled to put some distance between them so that she could see his face. "Ask *you* to give up everything! What's that supposed to mean?"

"Just what it sounds like," he half-smiled, his eyes locking with hers as she managed to turn her head a bit on the pillow. "Ask me to leave my job in Houston and move to Portland." He waited with a deceptively cool expression that totally confused Reva. What was he up to now?

"You just said you couldn't marry me if you didn't have a job," she reminded him carefully, warily.

"I said I couldn't ask you to marry me. A man has his pride," he added with a blandly disparaging smile. "But if you want me badly enough to ask me to give up everything I've worked for down in Houston and start a new life up here . . ."

"Josh Corbett, what the devil are you up to now?" Reva demanded, untangling herself from his embrace and maneuvering once again to a partially upright position. A position in which she was once again forced to grasp at the abused sheet. She pushed a handful of hair back behind her ear in an annoyed gesture.

He rolled over on his back, his lean body half uncovered

by the quilt, and watched her face perceptively. "It's easy enough to grasp," he told her calmly. "It's suddenly occurred to me that I'm going about this all wrong. A matter of tactics, honey. I'm appealing to you on two opposing fronts. I've just realized that I would do better to concentrate my firepower on your weakest point."

"Josh, if you don't stop talking to me in that horrible fashion, I swear, I'll . . ."

"Let me explain," he begged soothingly, placatingly. "On the one hand I've been throwing myself on your mercy and telling you to take me into your life. Then I turned right around and negated that appeal by telling you to come into *my* life. You see?" He waved a hand in mild annoyance. "I've weakened the strength of both attacks by aiming them at two different aspects of your nature. A simple, intelligent study of the matter dictates that I'm not approaching my goal in the most efficient manner. I should be aiming everything I've got at your most vulnerable barrier."

"Which is?" Reva demanded menacingly, not caring one bit for his newfound look of self-satisfaction. It was the same expression he'd worn when he'd brought back the first "liberated" chicken during their stay in South America. For some completely inexplicable reason the memory and the present situation combined to reach her sense of humor. Deliberately she squashed that reaction.

"Which is," he announced politely, grandly, "your inability to ignore weary, battle-scarred, and uncivilized males who've seen the light and want a home. Don't worry, honey," he added quickly, "I can fake my way through polite society even if I'm not as pretty and polished looking as Tanner. Like Xavier I can adapt to high-rise buildings and Mozart concerts. . . ."

"Mozart!" Reva repeated waspishly, not altogether certain why she grasped at that slender straw. "You lied to me about that, too? You don't like Mozart?"

"Darling, I've never had much exposure to classical music," he excused himself apologetically. "I've spent the past several years based in the Southwest, and I'm afraid that means country-western. . . ."

"And British-style mysteries?" Reva felt compelled to ask with a sense of righteous indignation. "Were you lying to me about liking that, too?"

He sighed, appearing vastly repentant. "I'm afraid I've been a science-fiction fan since I was nine years old."

"But you seem to know something about the subject," Reva heard herself protest. "I mean, when we watched television the other night you picked the British film . . ."

"I could tell by the way you read off the list of selections which one you wanted to see," he explained wryly. "I'm very good at reading the nuances in people's voices. It's a skill I've had to develop in my work."

"But, Josh, I distinctly remember not wanting to influence you in the matter. I tried to be quite neutral about it!"

"Which told me everything I needed to know," he grinned ruefully. "You were intent on being the perfect hostess to the sick visitor."

"You knew something about authors in the field," she insisted, not liking the idea that he had been able to manipulate her so easily.

"I'd been through your book and record shelf at odd moments, such as when you went shopping. All I had to do was glance through the brief biographies on the book jackets to pick up information I needed on authors."

"Another trick of your trade?" she grumbled.

"I'm afraid so."

"Josh, what is it exactly that you do for your company?" Reva asked with new suspicion.

"I'm a sort of troubleshooter, I guess," he admitted, watching for her reaction.

"A troubleshooter," she repeated with a frown, wondering how much territory that title covered.

"I've spent a lot of years coming and going in South and Central America," he elaborated patiently. "My firm uses me to deal with the local members of governments and the people who make financial decisions. I've got a lot of contacts and I know how to get past much of the incredible bureaucracy down there. Believe me, it's worse than our own!"

"You said you were the highest-ranking member on the scene when trouble broke out down there four months ago."

"I was." He didn't seem very interested in the discussion. "The firm has to give me a title to match the salary I get."

"And you're willing to give up this fantastic salary and title?" she prodded skeptically. He was trying to manipulate her again, she knew it. She just didn't know how to prove it!

"The moment you ask me to marry you," he returned immediately, cheerfully.

"I don't believe it." Her voice was flat, reflecting her certainty that no man would walk away from a high-paying position for the sake of a mere passing fancy. Or for any other reason, she added mentally.

"Try me," he invited smoothly. Too smoothly. Reva grew even more suspicious. What was he attempting to pull?

"Josh, you're absolutely incorrigible," she groaned, once more hauling the sheet around her and sitting up on

116

the edge of the bed. She flicked him a shuttered glance as she reached for her robe.

"I prefer to think of myself as persevering," he told her with only the smallest hint of arrogance. He turned on his side, watching almost wistfully as she hurriedly adjusted the robe around herself and stood.

Reva saw the expression, knew he wanted to ask her to stay, and knew, too, that she had to get back to the safety of her own room. She had to think, she decided, and she had to get Josh Corbett out from underfoot while she did it.

"There's not much use in running away, honey," he told her softly. "I'm going to continue the seduction routine. Sooner or later I'll find something that will work with you."

"I've told you I would never ask a man to give up everything for me," she muttered, realizing grimly that a part of her was intrigued. "Furthermore, modern as I like to think I am, I don't quite picture myself asking any man to marry me. There's a question of female pride involved, I think!" But she was aware that her words were spoken as much in challenge as in denial. It was as if she almost wanted to see what he would do, how he would counter next. Was she bent on testing him in some fashion? Was she trying to discover how badly he wanted a home with her? Even now, when he was demanding so much and trying so hard to make her accept him, he never spoke of love. She was a whim, a fixation, a temporary obsession. She had to remember that.

But how strong could an obsession like this become for a man who had probably spent too much time dealing with the rougher side of life? As strong as love might become for another man? Unconsciously she shook her head, telling herself not to become fanciful. Above all else Josh

Corbett was a most pragmatic, survival-oriented man. Such men did not spend long with short-term fancies. If they did they would not become high-paid troubleshooters for competitive energy firms!

"Then if you do wind up asking me to stay here in Portland," he told her deliberately, responding to her last words, "I'll know I've won completely, won't I? It will mean you've accepted the responsibility of me and that you've swallowed your own feminine pride." He slanted a glance upward at her, a glance which told her nothing of what he was really thinking.

She watched him for a moment in utter bemusement. "You never give up, do you?"

"Not when I want something badly enough," he agreed equably.

Reva drew a deep, steadying breath and made a strong mental effort to shake off the sensation of inevitability. "I can't stop you from hanging around my door, Josh Corbett," she began firmly.

"Just as you couldn't stop Xavier?" he chuckled.

"But I can put my foot down about having you in my apartment!" she concluded a little ruthlessly, feeling pressed.

"I should have stayed sick," he sighed, flopping back onto the pillows and closing his eyes briefly in disgust. "You're going to kick me out?" he asked, not opening his lashes. Those lashes, thought Reva inconsequentially, were much too long for a man. Especially for a man who had such a rock-hard face.

"Letting you stay would be admitting failure, wouldn't it?" she quipped dryly. "I can hardly do that at this point! And after hearing you admit to so many lies and attempts at manipulation, I would be a complete fool to allow you to continue to stay here!"

"You're not kicking me out because I allowed you a few misconceptions," he told her, shooting her a hooded glance from under the long lashes.

"Misconceptions!" she repeated, outraged at the euphemism.

"You're throwing me out," he continued bluntly, "because you're afraid you'll find yourself sneaking out here again tomorrow night."

"That's not true!" she hissed furiously, knowing full well it was. She was humiliated that she had shown herself so easily tempted by this man, but Reva told herself she would be damned if she would admit to it. "I happen to like my privacy. I only let you stay in the first place because I thought you were ill and because you pointed out that I owed you a favor. That wasn't very nice, Josh," she tacked on in annoyance.

"Forcing you to let me stay that first night by reminding you I'd saved your life? I was desperate." He lifted a hand, palm out in mute appeal. "Give me some credit. I didn't go on using that line. I switched to the sick routine as soon as I could."

"You will leave in the morning," she stated with a fine hauteur, lifting her chin regally.

"Okay," he agreed simply.

"Okay? Is that all you can say? You're not going to argue?" She stared at him in complete astonishment.

"Nope. I'll go." He paused significantly, eyeing her interestedly. "What's the matter? Did you want me to refuse?"

"Of course not!" she stormed. "I will say good-bye to you on my way to work!" Reva turned and headed for her own bedroom, not bothering to give him the satisfaction of a last backward glance. When she reached the protection of her room she shut the door behind her much too

119

gently. The small action, more than anything else, told an informed watcher how upset she really was. Xavier, curled comfortably in her bed, lifted his head with a questioning alertness that he wouldn't have bothered with if she'd slammed the door.

With a small groan of helpless despair Reva scrambled into bed beside the cat, asking herself over and over again what it was about the man in the other room which made her react in such a totally uncharacteristic fashion. It was as if there were some elemental contact which flowed between them regardless of any rational defenses she tried to implant in her mind. She was right to force him out of the apartment, Reva thought dismally. Having him under her roof would only lead to more incidents like tonight. She winced inwardly at the memory of how she had invited herself into his bed, throwing an arm over her eyes as if to shut out the mental picture.

Never had she found herself so weakened by a man, she acknowledged unhappily. Always before in her relationships she had been in control, just as she was in control around Bruce. Since her stupidity at the age of twenty-five she had taken great care to be the one controlling the situation, never letting the relationship control her.

But in the short time since his return to the States, Josh Corbett had easily managed to manipulate her in such an outrageous style that Reva didn't know whether to laugh or cry over her own idiocy. Tonight had been the turning point, though, she vowed silently, seethingly. She would force some physical distance between herself and Josh. Perhaps that would protect her until he tired of his infatuation with the dream of a home of his own.

Xavier very graciously got to his feet and padded up the hills and valleys of the quilt to touch his small nose to

Reva's chin. She reached out to stroke him reassuringly and attempted a small smile at the huge gray animal.

"I'll bet you're on his side, aren't you, cat?" she whispered wryly. "With your instinct for getting what you want, you probably appreciate a human being who works the same way you do! What is it that makes males like you and Josh pick on females like me? Are we such easy victims?" With a sigh Reva turned her face into the pillow and determined to sleep.

Although he was up ahead of her the next morning— even had the coffee on—there was no sign that Josh had started to pack his battered leather bag in preparation for moving out. His shaving things were stacked neatly in the bath and the suit he had worn the first night was still hanging in the hall closet. Reva noticed it when she opened the door to find her sleek red shoulder bag. Slung over the suit, she saw, was the brilliant crimson tie Josh had worn with it and the sight of it brought an unwilling smile to her lips.

She wiped the smile from her face before entering the kitchen and firmly stamped out the tiny flicker of feminine pleasure she experienced at the evidence of his presence around her. It would never do to let him stay, she reminded herself. For her own peace of mind Josh had to go.

He whistled as she swung around the corner and entered the kitchen. He had been reading the morning paper at the small table, a cup of coffee at his elbow. He was wearing a pair of casual, close-fitting slacks and a long-sleeved yellow shirt unbuttoned at the collar. There was an early-morning rakishness about him and an intimate, knowing gleam in the honey-colored eyes that brought a tide of warmth into Reva's cheeks.

"Dressed for work, lady, you are formidable indeed," he murmured appreciatively, sweeping the sight she made in the chic, tailored wool suit with its short jacket and slim skirt. Her heels were of a moderate, business-day height which unobtrusively accented well-shaped calves, and her hair was wrapped into a graceful but decidedly severe knot. The elegant glasses were perched firmly on her nose. "I like that scarf," he added, nodding at the bright scrap of silk at her throat.

Reva suddenly thought of his taste in neckties and was forced to smile. "I'm not surprised," she told him pertly, "I couldn't help but notice your tie the other night." She poured herself a cup of coffee.

"A real beauty, isn't it? I picked that up in Mexico City last year. Is that all you're going to have for breakfast?" he went on, brow darkening as he watched her drink her coffee standing at the counter.

"It's all I usually have when I'm working." She shrugged, not looking at him.

"Except when you have an excuse to splurge," he reminded her with gentle mockery. "Aren't you going to take advantage of my last morning here to have a proper meal?"

She glanced at him warily, thinking this morning represented one of the few times in her life when she wasn't interested in good food. A sign of the seriousness of the situation, she decided miserably.

"I'm not very hungry," she said quietly, and finished the coffee in silence.

"Perhaps by this evening you'll have regained your appetite," he consoled.

Reva lifted one eyebrow in a cool, repressive manner. "Meaning?"

He set down the paper and leaned back in the wicker and chrome chair, a considering look in the lion gaze.

"Meaning that I'm going to treat you to dinner, naturally."

"Are you?" she replied softly, a little dangerously. "But you'll be packed and gone by tonight, won't you, Josh?" She could feel the slight trembling in her fingertips and reached out to grasp the edge of the counter to still them. She prayed he hadn't noticed. Was he going to refuse to move out, after all?

"As you said last night, you can't keep me from hanging around your door, sweetheart," he drawled, seemingly unimpressed by her quelling look. "There's a price for my moving out without a fuss. Surely you expected that? You didn't really think I'd just slink off into the sunset, did you?"

"Why shouldn't I think exactly that?" she retorted, feeling baited by the taunting note buried in the gravelly voice. But privately she told herself she'd known it wasn't going to be easy. She ignored the other tiny voice which told her she hadn't wanted it to be easy.

"Because you're an intelligent woman who wouldn't make such a fundamental error as underestimating me."

"And the price is dinner?" Carefully she kept her voice even, not knowing whether to be relieved or dismayed by this turn of events. Josh had been right about one thing last night. Matters had been simpler back in the jungle. She hadn't begun questioning her feelings until she was safely home!

"Is that so high? Remember you'll be able to feel safe because you'll know I'm not going to be sleeping here tonight," he reminded her easily, and then cocked an inquiring brow. "Or are you afraid I shall put so much temptation in your path that you'll change your mind and beg me to stay?"

"You seem to have gained a rather false impression of

my self-control," she retorted tartly, rinsing her cup at the sink. He was deliberately challenging her and she knew it. But she didn't seem to be able to resist rising to the bait! "Don't be misled by what happened last night." She couldn't look at him as she referred to the events of the previous evening.

"Then if you're sure you have nothing to fear," he went on smoothly, "I'll pick you up at six thirty. Will that give you time to get home and changed for dinner?"

"Damn it, Josh, I haven't agreed to go out with you!" she began wrathfully, knowing full well she was going to lose this one. She turned the impact of a blue-green glare on him, her mouth tight at the corners, and waited for his arguments and demands. But all he said was,

"Please?"

Reva blinked, taken aback. She knew she was being manipulated again. Knew it and couldn't avoid it.

"You look," she told him blandly, "like Xavier when he's asking for a piece of the fish I'm preparing for my own dinner. Sort of wistful and hopeful. But you don't fool me for one minute. Either of you!"

"You know that if you don't grant the favor we're liable to sneak up and help ourselves anyway?" he grinned.

Reva drew a resigned breath. "All right, Josh, I'll go out with you. Provided you don't give me any trouble about moving out today!"

"You have my word on it," he promised at once.

"Umm," Reva muttered distrustfully, and then glanced at the clock. "I've got to be on my way. I have an early-morning staff meeting to conduct." She picked up her purse and raincoat on the way to the door and then paused, her hand on the knob. "Josh?"

"Yes, Reva?" he responded mildly, ambling across the

kitchen to lounge in the doorway, the coffee cup in his hand.

"Where will you go? Do you need a list of hotels or something?"

"A little late to be worrying about where I'll sleep tonight, isn't it?"

Reva turned without a word, her lips set in a firm line, and walked out the door. Let the alley cat find his own lodging!

What on earth, Reva asked herself several hours later as she took a small break at her desk, would she ever do without work? Nothing was as wonderfully useful for taking one's mind off personal problems, she decided with a rueful little grin. Carrying a cup of coffee over to the window, Reva studied the Portland skyline displayed beneath it. From here she could look across the Willamette River with its ten bridges pouring traffic back and forth. Her own tall apartment building was one of the many new structures clustered around the downtown core. Still small, as cities went, Portland had proven an ideal environment for Reva. A city she could call home. She found herself idly wondering if Josh ever thought of Houston as "home." A knock on her open door brought her attention back to business.

"Hello, Rick, what can I do for you?" she smiled at the front-line supervisor, one of four who reported to her, as she walked back to her desk. "Have a seat," she added, indicating a chair across from the desk.

"Thanks," he smiled back, accepting the offer. "I'm sorry to say I've got more bad news on the matter of trying to get that computer back up and running. The downtime is starting to add up and users are getting restless, to put it mildly."

"I thought you contacted the service people from the company two days ago," Reva frowned thoughtfully.

"I did and they promised they'd have someone out yesterday but no one showed," Rick Jameson groaned. "I'm afraid it's going to take a bit more clout than what I've got."

Reva nodded. "Okay, I'll see what I can do. Nothing makes people more irritable than a computer that's down." She punched the intercom on her desk and spoke quickly to her secretary, asking her to get the service department of the company from whom her firm rented the computer on the phone. Rick look quite relieved to be able to leave the matter in Reva's hands. He stood up to go, lifting a hand in thankful salute as he walked back out the door.

Within a matter of minutes Reva had the head of the service department on the line. A brief, firm chat got her nowhere and she hung up immediately. She wasted no more time but had her secretary put through a call to the business representative who had handled the original rental agreement.

"I'm afraid you heard me right, Mr. Hazelton," she was saying very kindly a bit later, "if you can't arrange to have your service department meet the terms of the agreement, I shall have the whole system yanked out lock, stock, and barrel by the end of the month. Your competition is already chafing at the bit to show us what they can do."

"Now, there's no need to be hasty," the business rep said at once, apparently realizing from the tone of her voice that Reva held some degree of real power. "I'll take care of everything."

"By this afternoon?"

"Definitely!"

By the time Reva was prepared to leave work the computer was once again on line, and when she checked on her way out, she found Rick Jameson humming happily in front of his console, working on a program.

"Everything all right, Rick?" she asked, pausing in the doorway.

"Perfect," he told her enthusiastically, glancing up. "Tape drive's functioning again and the printer is acting normally at last."

"Good," she nodded comfortably. "I'll see you in the morning."

It wasn't until she left the building that Reva allowed herself to really dwell on the coming evening. And when at last she did, the first thing she wondered about was what she would wear. Shaking her head at her own irrational behavior, she climbed into her BMW and headed for home.

The knock on her door came promptly at six thirty, as promised, and Reva found the palms of her hands damp with a strange nervousness as she went to open it. Josh had been as good as his word, she'd noted earlier. Every outward sign of his short stay had been removed, leaving no traces. She refused to speculate on the curious sense of depression which had overcome her as she'd walked into the apartment after work and found it looking as if he'd never been there. But now he stood at her door and she felt her spirits unaccountably lift. She must be crazy, Reva thought gloomily, glancing down at Xavier, who had bestirred himself to go with her to the door.

"It's a friend of yours," she told the cat dryly. "I'm sure you'll be glad to see him again!"

With a determined nonchalance Reva flung open her door and summoned a composed smile of greeting.

"Hello, Josh," she said politely, her eyes passing quickly over the well-cut but conservative suit he was wearing to center briefly on the spectacular, iridescent blue-green tie. "Come in, I'm almost ready."

"Thanks," he smiled cheerfully, scanning her deep royal-purple evening suit, and then he hesitated. "Wait a second," he told her. "I wore this tie to match your eyes but I think I've got something perfect for that suit!"

"Josh, wait a minute!" Reva managed, astonished. "Where are you going? You don't want to be bothered going all the way back to your hotel just to change a tie!"

"Won't take a second," he assured her cheerfully, fishing a key out of his pocket and fitting it into the lock of her neighbors' door. Without glancing back he disappeared inside, leaving an open-mouthed Reva staring after him.

"Hi, Reva," Sandy beamed, sticking her head around the door. "Saw Josh rushing back to his bedroom so I figured you'd be standing out here. You look fabulous!"

"His bedroom," Reva repeated blankly.

"Sure! We're glad to have him until you're ready to take him in permanently," her friend grinned, unabashed. "I can't tell you how much Tom enjoyed having a man to talk to today. . . . Oh, there you are, Josh," Sandy's auburn head turned to glance back down her hall. "Have a good time, you two. Don't worry, Josh, we won't wait up for you!" she chuckled, and shut the door behind him.

"Something wrong, sweetheart?" Josh asked politely, bending down briefly to scratch Xavier behind the ears and then moving into the room. The lion gaze laughed warmly down at her and Reva swallowed all her brilliant retorts.

"I've never," she said equally politely, "seen a purple necktie."

"Goes great with that suit, doesn't it?" he commented happily, glancing down at the bright item of apparel. "Are

128

you about ready? I'm starving. I thought we'd walk down to a place on the river that Tom and Sandy recommended. It's only a couple of blocks."

Reva said nothing as they descended in the elevator, but when Josh took her arm and guided her out through the lobby and onto the sidewalk, she finally found her tongue.

"Okay, Josh," she began in somewhat the same tone she'd used in dealing with the computer firm earlier in the day. "Let's have it." She pulled her coat collar up as a shield against the crisp night air. Fortunately it wasn't raining. "How did you manage to lodge yourself with Tom and Sandy?"

"Simple, really," he shrugged dismissingly. "I took Tom and Xavier for a walk today. . . ."

"A walk! You took Xavier?" she demanded in bewilderment.

"Sure. He sat in Tom's lap in the wheelchair until we reached the park and then he pretended to chase a few pigeons while Tom and I talked."

"About what?" Reva pressed ruthlessly.

"This and that."

"Josh!"

"Well, the truth is we sort of confided a bit in each other. Women aren't the only ones who do that, you know," he added aggressively. "I told Tom you were kicking me out. . . ."

"Oh, my God!" Reva groaned.

"And he told me about his problems."

"Being in the wheelchair?" Reva asked, a pang of sympathy for her neighbor going through her, in spite of more pressing problems.

"He's terrified he won't get out of it in another month, Reva," Josh told her quietly.

"But I thought it was all settled!"

129

"The odds are in his favor, but there's an outside chance something will go wrong."

"Does Sandy know?" she whispered.

"No, he hasn't told her, and he won't let the doctor tell her. He's been living with the fear for the whole time he's been in the chair. He's a man, Reva, he can face whatever he has to face, but it's the not knowing that's getting to him."

Reva said nothing for a moment, thinking of her neighbor's uncertain moods during the past two months. No wonder he'd been a little difficult for Sandy to deal with!

"Anyhow," Josh continued on a lighter note, "I think it did him good to talk to me about it."

"It probably did," Reva admitted softly, thinking that it had been very kind of her tormentor to spend the time with Tom. Her mouth curved slightly into an unconscious little smile at the mental image of Josh pushing Tom with Xavier in the other man's lap. She could just see the big cat sitting up straight and proud as if he owned the world. She felt herself soften once again toward the large man at her side. "And during the course of this rash of confidences, Tom invited you to stay with them?" she noted dryly.

"He's lonely during the day what with Sandy gone. Doesn't even have a cat or dog to keep him company. I think he liked the idea of having me around to talk to occasionally. And, naturally, he was very sympathetic to my plight," Josh tacked on in a melodramatic tone.

"I'll bet. Did you make me sound like a cold, hardhearted witch?" Reva's voice held an edge now.

"No," he grinned unrepentantly, "merely a slightly confused one."

"One of these days, Josh Corbett, I swear I'm going to lose my temper with you completely!"

"Is that a promise? I always enjoy it when you find yourself at the mercy of your emotions," he smiled. But there was a hint of warning in that smile and Reva contented herself with a glowering expression.

CHAPTER SEVEN

She should have been at least a little nervous about walking back to her apartment so late at night, Reva decided several hours later as Josh guided her back home, but somehow one didn't get nervous about things like that when he was around. His large, competent presence beside her made her feel as though she were being walked home by a tame lion.

"What's so funny?" Josh demanded, glancing down at her as she giggled suddenly.

"I was thinking of how you remind me of a lion. A sort of enlarged version of Xavier," she told him agreeably, wondering distantly if perhaps she'd had a bit too much to drink. The wine on their table had seemed never ending, she remembered. Was Josh resorting to the old trick of trying to get his date tipsy? That thought brought forth another chuckle and the man at her side smiled.

"I think we'd better stop for a little fresh air," he told her pleasantly.

"What do you mean stop for it? We're surrounded by it!" Reva gestured gracefully at the moonlit night overhead. "Sorry, Josh," she told him firmly, "you'll have to think of a better line than that!"

"How about stopping to view the fountains at the civic auditorium by moonlight? A fantastic view, I'm sure," he tried smoothly, leading her across a street toward the building in question. Across from the front of the auditorium a glorious fountain in the shape of several cascading waterfalls consumed a large portion of a city block.

"Well, that's somewhat more original, I suppose. You could always say we're stopping to absorb some of the negative ions. Aren't negative ions said to be produced in great abundance around waterfalls?" She tipped her face up to him in the streetlight, blue-green eyes full of humor. The evening had gone well, she thought warmly. Josh had seemed quite civilized, even sophisticated if you discounted the tie. He had a natural authority which immediately gained the services of maitre d's, waiters, and wine stewards in a way that Bruce Tanner would have envied.

"Let's find out if the ions are helpful in clearing away fumes from the head," he murmured. They stood at the top of the steps leading down to the fountain's pool and absorbed the spectacle for a moment in silence. The roar of water blanked out the sound of evening traffic and it seemed to Reva she was temporarily in another place and time. When Josh turned her slowly, pulling her against his warmth and solid strength, she went willingly, once again suspending common sense.

"Reva, my little gift from the jungle," he whispered, wrapping his arms around her and using his hand to press her head down onto his shoulder. "How long will it be before you're back in my bed?" When she would have stirred at his words, he held her more tightly, using the fingers at the nape of her neck to gently stroke until she quieted.

"Josh, please," she begged softly, turning her face into the fabric of his jacket. "Let's not talk about that. I behaved like a fool!"

"I haven't told you what last night meant to me," he

said deeply, lowering his head to kiss the back of her neck which was exposed by her upswept hair. "It was all I had been dreaming about for the past four months and more. Did you know that, sweetheart? Did you realize how my heart was pounding as I lay there listening to you come closer and closer to my bed?" His hand slid warmly down her back, coming to rest at the base of her spine, and he deliberately pressed her lower body against his thighs. Reva trembled slightly as she felt the hard, male swelling there. He felt her reaction and used his other hand to tilt her face upward.

"Oh, Josh," she breathed helplessly as his mouth came down on hers. Then, telling herself she was safe out here in the open, Reva let herself respond to the compelling, demanding fire of his kiss. This man never did anything by halves, she thought fleetingly. When he kissed her he brought to bear all the reserves housed in a man's arsenal. She was made to know the range and depth of his need as he exposed her to every point of the spectrum of his methods for getting what he wanted.

Again she shivered as his mouth fully involved hers, now challenging, now pleading, now demanding, and now taking. She felt her hands sliding inside the warmth of his jacket almost against her will. But, then, she didn't seem to have much will when Josh took her into his arms.

At the touch of her hands on his back a tremor seemed to go through Josh. Reva felt it along the length of her body pressed so close to his, and his kiss deepened. His tongue forged briefly into her mouth and then he caught her lower lip between his teeth and bit with a gentle violence that seemed to stoke the fire in her nerve endings.

"Take me home, Reva," he urged huskily, straining her against him. "Take me home and let me make love to you the way I did last night. I want you!"

135

Reva heard herself cry out in a small whimper of pleasure-pain as his mouth moved along the line of her jaw to her earlobe and continued its punishment. He heard the cry and instantly his tongue came forth to soothe the area his teeth had been erotically savaging. As soon as she relaxed once more against him he resumed the delicate, merciless attack until Reva thought she would collapse in a dizzying world of sensation. His coercive lovemaking emboldened an underlying desire to retaliate in kind and Reva began to return the tender assault.

With deliberate wantonness she sank her nails into the skin of his back, the material of his shirt providing little protection, and when he groaned hoarsely in response she parted her lips and nipped lightly along the length of his throat.

"Reva!" he growled thickly. "I can't take much more of this. You're driving me out of my mind, witch!"

"I thought," she whispered daringly, feeling very much the witch he had labeled her, "that you could take almost anything, Josh. Aren't you the man who gets sent in to handle what others can't? Aren't you the one who kept me alive for three days in the middle of a revolution?" She moved against him deliberately, safe in the knowledge that they were in a public spot and that no matter how much she tempted him or he tempted her nothing could come of it. "Don't tell me there's anything you can't deal with, Josh Corbett," she taunted, wondering at her own courage.

"You're very brave tonight," he said quite silkily. "Why is that, I wonder? Do you want to see how far you can push me?" His hands slid lower on her hips, melding her against him in an audacious way that made her catch her breath. "Go ahead, little Reva. See how close you can play to the edge. . . ." He inhaled the fragrance of her hair as

136

he spoke. "Since I've returned I've allowed you to take the final initiative. I've played the part of supplicant, asking for you, pleading for you, but not taking you until you finally asked me to last night. But I could try other approaches, Reva, my sweet. Approaches that would have you shivering helplessly in my arms whether or not you wanted it that way!" There was faint humor beneath the warning timbre of his voice but it didn't disguise the intent in him. Reva abruptly realized she was, indeed, playing a very dangerous game.

Prudently she began to pull away from him, smiling as she did so to show she wasn't genuinely frightened. Her sea eyes sparkled up at him from behind the safety of her lenses and she knew she was still caught up a bit in the excitement and tantalization of the moment.

"That's enough!" she whispered on the top of a smothered laugh. "I'm quite terrified, Josh. I wouldn't dream of trying your patience too far."

"I don't mind," he assured her, gazing down at her with eyes that still held the fire of a moment before. "I only felt duty bound to let you know there were limits."

"Are there truly?" she mocked softly, smiling at him.

"Yes," he said simply.

"Ah, well," she sighed, twisting out of his arms and starting back up the steps. "So much for a lovely evening."

He took the steps two at a time and reached out to snag her hand, holding it firmly as they continued on toward the apartment. "Did you really enjoy it, Reva?" he asked after a moment.

"Yes," she said honestly, "I did."

"You see?" he grinned, a slashing, buccaneering grin, "I can fake my way through a social engagement when called upon to do so."

"Were you faking, Josh?" she asked softly, thinking

how the conversation had flowed easily between them at dinner. He was an intelligent man who had seen a great deal of the world and she had to admit she had found their first real dinner out together fascinating.

"No," he told her just as softly, the fingers holding her hand squeezing slightly tighter, "I was enjoying myself courting the woman I'm going to marry."

"So it's become a courtship now instead of a seduction?" she couldn't help retorting.

"Same thing," he said with that familiar, massive shrug. "Tomorrow night I'm going to amaze and confound you with my culinary talents. Think how pleasant it will be to walk in the door after work and find dinner waiting for you along with a drink."

Reva took a breath. "I can't tomorrow night, Josh. I have a date." She didn't look at him as she spoke. Instantly the atmosphere between them chilled.

"Tanner?" he asked in an enigmatic tone.

"We're attending a social function being given by a business club to which he belongs," she explained, wondering in confusion how she wanted him to react to the news. What was wrong with her? she thought irritably.

There was a long, drawn-out silence and then Josh said very calmly, "I can't let you do that, Reva. It was hard enough on Sunday night when I knew you'd be returning home and I'd be waiting to make sure he didn't try to claim you. I can't go through it again." He wasn't looking at her, focusing instead on the pattern of lights visible in the windows of her building.

"I'm sorry, Josh, but I can't cancel the engagement. And . . . you don't own me," she concluded in a voice barely above a whisper.

"Yes," he said briefly, "I do."

"Don't talk like that," she ordered quickly, glancing

warily up at his rough-hewn face. They were in the lobby now, heading for the elevators. "You know it's not true!"

He said nothing, just looked at her. And in that look was all the masculine promise in the world. It blazed out at her from the depths of the catlike eyes, telling her without words that Josh had claimed her for his own, that she would deny that claim only at her peril. The soft magic of the evening dissolved in a flash and beneath it she once again saw the hard, unrelenting pursuer intent on possession. But something in her refused to back away from the challenge.

"Good night, Josh," she said quietly as they stepped from the elevator. "And thank you for dinner."

"Reva . . ." he began, and then bit off his own words with a low growl. "What's the point of talking?" He caught hold of her shoulders and hauled her against him, locking her mouth to his in a short, savage kiss that echoed the primitive gleam in his eyes. Then he set her aside, opened her door, and pushed her into the darkened hall of her apartment. Without a word he closed the door in her face. A moment later she heard him letting himself into Sandy and Tom's apartment. She'd just had, instinct told her, something of a narrow escape.

It was the delightful cooking odors seeping out from under her door that alerted Reva the next evening as she returned home from work. There was only one person in the world who would have the gall to use her kitchen without permission, she told herself morosely as she let herself inside.

"In here, Reva!" Josh's voice came cheerfully from the direction of the kitchen.

"Sandy and Tom aren't feeding you well enough?" she inquired blandly, coming to lean with crossed arms in the doorway. He was busily checking something which simmered appealingly in a large oven pot. His sleeves were rolled up to his elbows and a towel was tucked into his belt as an apron. She wanted to smile at the picture he made and didn't dare. Josh, as usual, was up to mischief. It only remained to be seen what sort.

"Sandy and Tom," he corrected, glancing up with a smile, "have fed me most graciously. I'm having them over tonight."

"I see," she nodded, one brow lifting as she peered suspiciously at him through her glasses. "Felt like doing a little entertaining, is that it?"

"That's it." He straightened, closing the oven door and twisting around behind him to pick up a glass off the counter. "Here you go. As promised, a welcome-home drink." He pushed it toward her and Reva found herself having to take it.

"How did you get into the apartment, Josh?" she demanded in the most casual of voices, ignoring Xavier, who was strapping himself slowly, languidly around her ankles. He didn't mind being ignored. His main attention was focused on Josh's cooking.

"With the key you gave to Tom and Sandy, naturally," he said, appearing surprised at her slow thinking. "I used it yesterday to get Xavier."

She nodded, taking a small sip of her drink while she tried to think through the various possibilities in the situation. "Smells good," she commented dryly.

"My one perfected party dish," he grinned. "Stew." He was engaged in pulling dishes out of the cupboard.

"Stew?"

"Well, in some places it's called boeuf Bourguignon," he admitted, "but I've always thought of it as stew."

"Do you, uh, entertain a great deal?" she couldn't resist asking.

140

"Not much. Hence the development of only one dish," he chuckled. "You're welcome to join us, Reva," he said, looking very much as if he was afraid she might be feeling left out.

Reva wanted to laugh at the innocent expression on his face. Josh was not good at innocent expressions, but she was beginning to feel mildly alarmed.

"Thank you, but as you may recall, I have other plans," she reminded him pointedly, stirring the ice in her drink with a fingertip.

"Ah, yes," he nodded as if he'd forgotten. "What time is Tanner picking you up?" He carried his stack of dishes past her to the dining table which occupied a special end of the living room.

"In about half an hour." And then Reva smiled very kindly, unable to resist the next remark. "But you needn't worry about him interrupting your entertaining. I've told him to buzz me from the lobby intercom and I'd come on down to meet him." That, she had told herself during the day, had been a stroke of genius. She didn't really believe that even Josh would do something terribly drastic if she encountered Bruce in the hall outside her door, but it was better to be safe than sorry.

"No problem," he told her, hovering about the dining-room table as he adjusted the silverware and dishes. "Thanks for letting me use your place, by the way."

"Think nothing of it," she grumbled. "Make yourself right at home!" As soon as she said the words she could have bitten her tongue.

"Thank you. I will." No inflection at all in the deep voice.

There was no adequate response to that, so Reva took herself off to her bedroom to change.

Half an hour later she was again standing in the kitchen

doorway, this time wearing a white wool skirt and black velvet blazer, and counting the seconds until the intercom would announce Bruce's presence in the lobby. She was watching Josh put the finishing touches on his salad when a knock came at the door. Startled, Reva turned, wondering if Bruce had forgotten the arrangement. What a fiasco that would be, she thought gloomily, imagining herself trying to explain Josh in her kitchen.

"I'll get it," Josh said immediately, moving ahead of her. "That will be Tom and Sandy. They were due a couple of minutes ago."

Reva relaxed slightly and then frowned, glancing at her watch. Bruce was normally very much on time. Perhaps she should go on down to the lobby and wait for him. And then a gray chill washed through her as she heard Josh's voice at the door.

"Hello, Tanner. I'm afraid Reva can't come out and play tonight. Or any other night, for that matter." His tone was cold, smooth, and deliberately taunting. "I know you want her but it's too late. She already belongs to me and has for the past four months!"

"Josh!" Reva gasped, horrified. She hurried toward the door on legs that felt suddenly weak around the knees. "How dare you . . ." She was forced to come to an abrupt halt because he was blocking the entrance with his body. She had a vague glimpse of Bruce Tanner's astonished and angry face just before the younger man spoke.

"Reva! What the hell is going on here? You told me your *guest* was well and had moved out!" The narrowing blue eyes went quickly from Josh's coolly uncompromising expression to Reva's stunned face.

"Bruce, don't listen to him! He's only trying to create trouble."

Josh moved, forcing Bruce back into the hall without

touching him. "The bit about being sick was something of a small ruse, I'm afraid," he said in bland apology. "I needed a reason to spend the weekend, you see." He was still advancing on a slowly, angrily retreating Bruce. Josh made no overt move to menace the other man, but the slow, casual pacing was violence incarnate. Reva began to panic, at a loss to know how to deal with the situation.

"Josh, stop it this minute!" she ordered. "Bruce, go on downstairs. I'll be right behind you!"

But Bruce wasn't listening to her. His handsome features were twisting into the resentful expression of a man who feels himself badly humiliated.

"I don't know what you think you're doing, Corbett," he announced grandly, coming to a halt and looking very much as if he intended to stand his ground. "But you're not going to get away with it!"

"Reva's mine," Josh said very softly. "Whose arms do you think she slept in that night after you brought her home from the concert? And that's not the first time."

Reva gave into the urge to panic. This was beyond her. She needed the help of another man. Unthinkingly she pounded on Tom and Sandy's door. The sound of Bruce and Josh's voices grew increasingly dangerous and when Tom answered the door in his wheelchair Reva nearly collapsed into his lap.

"Tom," she begged desperately. "You've got to do something! They're going to fight! Josh has gone crazy and . . ."

Tom glanced beyond her to the two men standing near the elevator. His eyes narrowed thoughtfully and then he gestured for Reva to get out of the way. She stepped aside as Sandy came into the hall, a worried look on her face.

"Reva! What is it? What's going on?"

"There isn't time to explain," Reva began, watching s

Tom approached the other two men and then halted his chair. "Josh is behaving like . . . like an animal and poor Bruce . . ."

At that moment Bruce Tanner clearly appeared to have taken enough of Josh's goading intimidation. The sight of other witnesses to his humiliation must have pushed him over the brink.

As Reva and her neighbors watched, stunned, the younger man swore violently and swung his clenched fist in an arcing curve.

"My God!" Reva heard herself say in a terrified whisper, "Josh will kill him!" She started forward but Sandy caught her arm and then they watched as the blow connected with the edge of Josh's jaw.

Bruce looked quite as startled as the others when Josh collapsed to the hallway carpet with a groan.

For a moment the entire group seemed frozen in a tableau and then Reva broke the spell, racing forward to where Josh lay very still on the floor.

"Josh!" she cried, sinking to her knees beside him. There was blood on his mouth. "Josh! Are you all right?" There was no answer and the lion eyes remained closed. But he stirred vaguely.

"How long did you think you could play me for the fool, Reva?" Bruce finally found his tongue to ask, straightening his jacket and tie with a new arrogance. "You can only push a man so far," he told her grimly. "I suggest you think twice before you try playing two men off against each other again!" Turning, he stabbed the elevator button with great force. Fortunately for the grand exit he seemed intent on making, the elevator responded almost immediately. The doors slid open, Bruce stepped inside, and they closed on his expression of masculine hauteur. It was an expression Reva had never seen on his face before and she could only stare at the closing elevator doors in shock.

At that moment another apartment door farther down the hall opened and the lawyer who lived in 18C stuck his silver head out. "Trouble?" he inquired blandly, taking in the sight of the others.

"Nothing we can't handle, Harold, thank you," Tom retorted, moving his chair forward with great authority and reaching over the side to grasp Josh's arm. "Reva," Tom continued, flicking a stern glance at her still-stunned face. "Go with Sandy. I'll get Josh taken care of."

Reva's gratitude showed in her eyes as she got shakily to her feet and stumbled toward the waiting Sandy. Behind her she heard Tom speaking to a now groaning Josh.

"Come on, hero. Let's get you cleaned up!"

With a firm hand on her upper arm Sandy hauled Reva into the apartment while Tom guided Josh into Reva's.

"Calm down, Reva," Sandy crooned soothingly, leading her friend into the living room and pushing her gently onto the couch. "Everything's going to be fine. Tom will get your man back into shape and we can all sit down to a nice dinner."

"I have never been so appalled in my life, Sandy," Reva interrupted, shaking her head from side to side in disbelief. "How could he have allowed such a thing to happen?"

"Who? Bruce or Josh?" Sandy retorted.

"Either of them! But I suppose I was most surprised at Bruce. I never thought of him as a violent man. Did you see him when he got on the elevator? He looked positively arrogant! I couldn't believe it." Reva lifted a still-shaking hand to her hair, pushing it unconsciously back into place in its neat knot. "What a scene! I was so humiliated! And the blood on Josh's face!"

"It's all right, Reva. I'm sure Josh will be fine."

"I could strangle him and Bruce both!"

"Well, you can take consolation from the fact that Bruce seems to have clobbered Josh pretty soundly," Sandy half-smiled, eyeing her friend curiously. "At least one of them was punished."

"You know, that surprised me a bit," Reva admitted, sinking back into the couch to gaze blindly out the window. "Somehow I would have imagined Bruce as the one getting clobbered if anyone had suggested a fight between the two."

"Josh probably didn't expect Bruce to lose control that far. I certainly didn't!" Sandy said feelingly. "Who would have thought a nice, polite man like that would be reduced to taking a swing at another man?"

Reva got to her feet with determination. "I'm going to see how Tom's getting along with Josh. I hope there are no lost teeth," she muttered, thinking of the blood. What a ghastly mess, literally and figuratively! Reva went quickly out the door, aware of Sandy following more slowly. The door to her own apartment still stood partially open and she slipped quietly inside, hearing noises from the direction of the bathroom. She really would give Josh Corbett a piece of her mind when this was all over, she told herself, but first she would make certain he was all right. The thought of him being hurt sickened her in a nearly physical way that she couldn't fully understand.

She moved silently down the hall on the plush carpeting and stopped just before rounding the bathroom door. Tom was speaking calmly with a distinctly dry note in his voice.

"I think you're going to live, pal. No serious damage at any rate."

"It wouldn't matter if there were. Reva's not going to marry me for my good looks!" Josh growled.

"Was it worth it?"

146

"Sure," Reva heard Josh reply easily over the sound of running water. "Tanner got to keep his pride and I got to keep Reva. A fair exchange." Reva could almost see the familiar lifting of one shoulder in a dismissing shrug and her fingers closed into small fists at her side.

"I couldn't believe it when I saw you deliberately step into that wide swing and then fake that grand collapse to the floor. Very effective," Tom said with a touch of genuine admiration.

"What do you mean, deliberately?" Josh retorted, sounding offended. "The guy's a lot younger than me and I . . ."

"And you're a hell of a lot faster and meaner," Tom interrupted bluntly. "Don't try and tell me you didn't plan the whole thing exactly as it happened."

Josh sighed. "The hard part was getting him to take a swing at all. For a while there I thought he'd simply leave in a huff and I'd wind up looking the villain of the piece. . . ." He broke off as he glanced into the mirror, his hand pausing in the act of dabbing the cut on his lip. "Hello, Reva, honey. Come to comfort the wounded?" The lion eyes looked abruptly wary.

Reva, who had moved to stand in the doorway, met his gaze in the mirror and felt like reaching for the nearest available weapon.

"Not only did you start the fight," she began on a low snarl, wishing he weren't so much bigger than herself—she would dearly love to curl her fingers around his throat and squeeze—"but you set poor Bruce up, didn't you? That was the sneakiest, most underhanded, conniving thing I have ever witnessed!"

"Come on, now, sweetheart," he murmured cajolingly, his eyes still cautious, "for a while there you actually felt

147

sorry for me, didn't you? I figured a woman like you would head for the side of the underdog."

"The underdog!" she snapped, infuriated at once again having been well and truly manipulated. "Why you arrogant, deceitful . . ."

"Please, dear, not in front of the neighbors," he said wryly, reaching with great casualness for her hairbrush on the counter as she took a step forward.

"Oh, don't mind us," Tom instructed, a grin tugging at the corners of his mouth as he surveyed the two.

"Oh, but we must," Josh objected, still watching Reva's tense face in the mirror and still holding the brush. "Reva hates scenes. Sweetheart," he went on evenly, "why don't you go wait out in the living room with Sandy? I promise I'll let you yell at me all you like after dinner. Right at the moment my temper is a shade uncertain, however, and I'm not quite in the mood for a lecture."

Reva stared at him, finding herself horrifyingly torn between two opposite reactions. The first was anger but the second, disconcertingly enough, was a simple desire to surrender to the inevitable. Josh Corbett certainly had to rank as the most outrageous male she had ever encountered in her life. How could you fight someone like this? Her eyes went speculatively to the hairbrush he was holding and back to meet his gaze. "Until after dinner, then," she drawled coolly, turning on her heel and walking out.

"I thought she'd see it my way," she heard Josh tell Tom. Reva ground her teeth in response. After dinner she was going to tear a wide strip off that man if it was the last thing she ever did, she vowed silently.

"Do I take it you'll be joining us for dinner?" Sandy asked, clearly trying to keep a straight face as she watched her friend exit the bathroom in favor of the living room.

"I wouldn't miss it for the world," Reva told her with

great depth of feeling. "I've been granted a license for mayhem immediately following, you see."

The meal went off, amazingly enough, with great perfection. Josh's fancy "stew" was a masterpiece and Reva's normal appetite returned in a rush when he carried it out to the table. He played the host with great enthusiasm, pouring wine from Reva's small store with a lavish hand. But perhaps the most redeeming feature of the evening was Tom's lighthearted and genuinely cheerful mood. The happy look in Sandy's eyes every time she glanced at her husband was worth a great deal, Reva thought. And there was no doubt that Josh was the cause of it. This evening's adventure seemed to have deepened an already strong friendship. She sighed to herself, wondering what Bruce had done after leaving the building. She realized with a pang that she wasn't brokenhearted at the obvious rift in her relationship with the man. In fact, it was hard to think of him at all. It was much easier to think of Josh and all the things she was going to say to him when dinner was finished.

It was much later, as Sandy was preparing to leave with Tom, that she took Reva aside and smiled gratefully at her. "Thank you, Reva."

"For what?" Reva asked in surprise.

"For letting the evening go along so nicely. You had every right to make it a miserable occasion for everyone!" she assured her neighbor understandingly.

"My time," Reva promised smoothly, "is coming."

"Don't be too hard on him, Reva, he meant well."

"He *meant,*" Reva corrected with great emphasis, "to get his own way. As usual."

"He is a bit different from the ordinary, run-of-the-mill male, isn't he?" Sandy grinned. "Tom likes him a lot and he's usually an excellent judge of character. Well, we, uh,

149

won't wait up for him," she concluded meaningfully. "See you later, Reva."

The door closed behind her and her husband as they headed back to their own apartment.

Reva waited a long, considering moment after seeing her friends out before joining Josh in the kitchen. He was busily stacking dishes into the dishwasher and running a sinkful of sudsy water. He glanced up with an expression of resigned patience as she came to stand beside him, her hands on her hips.

"Should I be sitting down for this?" he asked her politely, straightening. The lion eyes gleamed as he absorbed her attitude of determination.

"Suit yourself," she bit out with mocking politeness.

"Thank you. I'll take the couch." Without a word he led the way back into the living room and sprawled on the red sofa, watching her with a narrowed look. Xavier, sensing something of passing interest, trotted over and took up a position on the back of the expensive piece of furniture where he would have a good view.

"Do I get to state my side of the case first?" Josh inquired blandly.

"I've already heard your side of the case," Reva announced equally blandly, beginning to pace back and forth in front of the huge expanse of windows. "I saw the whole thing, remember? You deliberately goaded the man I had intended to marry, saying unkind things about me in the process. . . ."

"I only let him know you'd slept with me," he pointed out with a quirking smile.

"Perhaps the unkindest thing of all," Reva said softly, stopping to gaze out at the night-darkened city. "A gentleman, Josh, would not have done such a thing." Her voice was suddenly very bleak as she thought about her words.

"Gentlemen, I will agree, do not discuss casual affairs with other men," he told her smoothly. "But it is a slightly different matter when marriage is involved. At that point it becomes very important to let other men know the territorial limitations, and there is no surer way than letting them know the full extent of the relationship."

"You are an arrogant, conceited, and thoroughly unprincipled man! You don't deserve the home you claim to want!"

"I know," he said softly. "But we seldom get what we deserve in this world, only what we want badly enough."

"You must want it very badly," she shot back, whirling to glare at him, "to humiliate and disgrace me in front of someone I liked a great deal. I hope you enjoyed yourself, Josh. Did you derive a special satisfaction from knowing how you made me look?"

"I only let him know he couldn't have you, sweetheart," Josh said placatingly. "Was that so bad? After all, it's the truth."

"It is not the truth! You have no rights over me, Josh Corbett, in spite of what you may think. The man I marry will be a gentleman and if there was any doubt about your gaining that status there isn't any longer. Never have I seen a more disgusting display of outrageous, ungentlemanly behavior in my life!"

"Hey, wait a minute," he protested. "It was Tanner who took a swing at me, not vice versa!"

"Egged on by you!"

"I only put him in possession of the facts! Furthermore, you can't say you weren't warned! What happened this evening was all your own fault!"

"My fault!" Reva heard her voice rising on a small shriek.

"I told you last night I couldn't let you go out with him.

151

Did you really think I didn't mean it or were you just testing me to see if I could enforce my instructions?"

Reva stared at him, shocked. My God! she thought blankly. Had she done such a thing, even unconsciously? Her inner self-doubts were mirrored in her eyes before she could control her reaction to the accusation, and Josh saw it. In an instant he was on his feet, moving toward her with that catlike, pacing stride.

"That's it, wasn't it?" he growled softly, reaching out to snag her by the shoulders and haul her close. "You wanted to see how much you could get away with tonight, didn't you?"

"No!" she defended herself furiously, struggling and failing to free her body from his rasp. All of a sudden it was she who was on the d ensive and she could have kicked herself for allowing it to happen. A basic managerial mistake, she thought angrily. "I deliberately arranged to meet him in the lobby so that you wouldn't run into him, even accidentally!"

"You were just trying to make things difficult for me," he disagreed. "And in any event, I foresaw that little maneuver. Why do you think Tanner came knocking on your door?"

"What did you do, damn it?" she blazed.

"I turned off your intercom box. He probably did try to buzz you and came on up when he couldn't get through!"

Reva gave into the overriding impulse to slap him, lifting her hand to bring it with all her might across his cheek. Never had she been angrier with herself and with a man.

But the blow never landed. Josh *was* fast, she realized dimly as he caught her wrist. Tom had been right. The lion's gaze darkened with warning.

"Sorry about that, Reva," he mocked grimly, "but one roundhouse punch is all I'm in the mood to take tonight!"

In the next instant he had twisted her wrist behind her back, not causing her any pain, but totally immobilizing it. Then, before she quite realized what was happening, he swept her into his arms, going down on one knee. In another second she was flat on her back against the thick, luxurious carpet and he was lowering his heavy strength against her, trapping her there.

"I think," he said very distinctly, "that it's time you consoled the poor loser of tonight's heroic battle!"

CHAPTER EIGHT

For the first time since she had met Josh Corbett, Reva knew a sense of fear. She had felt many things around this man, she acknowledged as she gazed up at him with widened eyes—gratitude, compassion, annoyance, outrage, humor, and dismay—but she had never known fear before now.

"Josh! No!" she gasped as she absorbed the full impact of his weight along the length of her body. "Not like this! You've never forced me like this!"

"I warned you last night there were limits, Reva," he grated, his fingers going ruthlessly to the buttons of her blouse. She had removed her blazer earlier when it became obvious she wasn't going out for the evening.

Reva struggled, still angry from the argument which had gone before and now battling the surge of fear. "Let me go," she hissed, slapping ineffectually at his hands as they went rapidly from one button to the next. "I won't let you do this to me! Why are you behaving like this? You won tonight, didn't you? You've ruined my relationship with Bruce!" He was pushing the blouse off her shoulders, pulling on the sleeves to remove it completely. She could see only a masculine vengeance and determination in the honey-lion eyes and her heart skipped a beat at what it portended.

"A man can get awfully damn tired of waiting for his woman to come to her senses!" he snapped, slinging the blouse off to the side and reaching for the zipper of her skirt. "How much longer did you think I'd be content to let you play your little games? Content with taking your little handouts whenever it pleased you to throw them in my direction? I told you that first night there would be hell to pay if you dragged another man between us but you had to go and push too hard, too often!" He had her skirt off completely and was attacking her beige undergarments without any regard for the fine lacy fabric.

Reva wedged her hands against his chest, pushing at him with all her power, but he was too heavy; much too heavy. Already her breath was coming more quickly from the exertion of fighting him. Soon she would be exhausted.

"Please, Josh," she begged. "Stop it! Do you want me to hate you?"

He sucked in his breath, staring down at her as he removed the last of her garments. "You won't hate me," he told her in a soft, grim voice. "You can't hate me. Deep down you want me as much as I want you. Do you think I've learned nothing from the times you spent in my arms?"

His hands were sliding over her body, searching out the curve of her shoulder, the swell of her small breast, the contour of her waist and the promise of her thigh. His fingers were possessive, probing things that had learned her well in the past and knew many of the secret places which responded to his touch. He began to exert his mastery of her with calculated, marauding power.

Reva twisted beneath him, trying desperately to find some room for movement. Her head moved restlessly from side to side on the carpet, destroying the design of her hair and tousling it into a sun-streaked mass of softness. She felt her glasses almost torn from her face and then her head was caught and held between Josh's palms as he lowered his mouth to hers.

"I'm through pleading for your warmth, Reva," he husked against her lips. "Tonight I'm going to take what's mine. Did you think I'd be satisfied waiting patiently for you to condescend to visit my bed again?" His lips ground against her mouth so fiercely she could feel his teeth collide with her own.

When he raised his head again, her lips were bruised and the inside of her mouth felt ravaged. Still lying squarely on top of her crushed body, Josh raised the upper part of his torso and began yanking his shirt out of the waistband of his slacks. His eyes never left hers as he efficiently scrambled out of the shirt, hurling it from him impatiently. When he came back down on her, it was with a low groan of need. Reva felt the buckle of his belt digging into the skin of her stomach at the same instant her breasts were unmercifully scraped by the coarse hair of his chest.

She cried out softly when he drove his knee between hers, creating a space for himself between her legs that left her feeling helpless and ravished.

"Damn you, Josh! Leave me alone! You have no right to treat me like this! I've done nothing to you!"

"Nothing except force me to beg outside your door when I should be inside."

"What makes you think you can take anything you want, even me?" she managed, panting heavily with the effort she was making. With her heel she tried to kick at his leg but he ignored the small pain she dealt him.

"What made you think you had any right to encourage another man when you belonged to me?" he countered furiously. "I've been too patient with you; too gentle!"

Reva had a brief glimpse of the fire glittering in his eyes

before he bent his head to toy with small savagery at her breasts. She felt his lips and then his teeth tugging at first one nipple and then the other while his hands held hers out to the side. There was damp heat on her stomach when he interrupted the passionate capture of her breasts to kiss her lower down.

Then he was moving, shifting himself to the side and pulling her until she lay facing him. His leg still lay across hers, still trapping her, but his hands began to work down the length of her back, digging into her small, feminine muscles from the base of her neck to the curve of her hip. It was like some sort of rough, erotic massage and Reva felt herself tremble in response.

No, she thought in shock, she must not let herself surrender to him under these conditions. She realized with dim, blind instinct that it wasn't only herself who would suffer from the consequences but also Josh. She didn't know how she knew and she didn't bother to question why she cared. She was only aware that she had to stop him before he had gone too far and reaped a harvest of regret.

"Josh," she whispered appealingly, no longer struggling but using her one free hand to stroke his hair much as she would have stroked Xavier. "Josh, please, listen to me. It won't be any good for either of us like this. You must realize that. I know you don't want to hurt me. You've never hurt me." Desperately she kept talking, her fingers rifling through the gray wings of his hair in long soothing gestures. She could still feel his rough hands on her skin but there was a difference now. A difference that was reflected in his eyes. She felt a shudder go through his hard frame as she talked.

But quite suddenly Reva wasn't at all sure she liked the expression which was replacing the arrogant, demanding male one which had been in those eyes. For this new look was one of gathering pain and it was like a sword in its effect on her.

"Reva," he breathed heavily, his hands stilling on her body. "Reva, my little one, God forgive me! I never meant to hurt you!" She saw the clouds form in the honey-colored eyes and she wanted to cry herself. She sensed his rising self-disgust and wanted to stem it even though she knew it was her ticket to freedom. All she had to do was fail to respond to that masculine pain, to show herself fearful and angry, and Josh would drag himself out of her apartment. She was sure of it.

"I know, Josh," she whispered, a small, womanly smile on her lips. "I know." Almost unconsciously her fingers continued their stroking of his hair.

"I . . . I don't know what got into me," he muttered, rolling abruptly over onto his back and staring blankly at the ceiling. "Something seemed to snap inside when you tried to hit me. Everything came to a boil and all I could think about was ending this stupid game we're playing once and for all." He swore a short, harsh oath. "What you must think of me tonight! And I had it all so beautifully planned!" This last was said with such abject self-pity that Reva felt a surge of very female humor.

"Did you really, Josh?" she said with a new lightness, watching as he rubbed his eyes in a gesture of weary disgust. At her tone he dropped his hand from his face and turned his head to look at her.

"Are you laughing at me, Reva Waring?" he growled after a moment, his long lashes partially concealing the depths of his eyes.

"And if I am?" she mocked gently, lifting a hand to touch his shoulder with lazy fingers. Anything, even a resurgence of his temper, was better than the self-pity and disgust he was experiencing.

"I deserve it, I guess," he sighed.

"Oh, I don't know," she grinned, her blue-green eyes gleaming with humor. "You've been through a great deal tonight. The least I could be is understanding!"

"True," he agreed wryly, slanting an enigmatic look at her.

Reva laughed, shaking her head. "You're utterly impossible. You know that, don't you? I've never met anyone like you in my life. I wanted to throttle you tonight when you pulled that stunt with poor Bruce and then I wanted to thank you for what you're doing for Tom. He looked better tonight than he has since the accident. Sandy's quite put you on a pedestal because of that. You save my life only to throw it into absolute chaos. What am I going to do with you?"

"You could take me into your life," he suggested instantly. "Once I'm there I'm sure everything would settle back down to normal!"

"You're so very sure that's what you want, Josh?" she whispered, the laughter fading from her tone as she studied him with new intentness. His obsession with a home seemed as strong as ever, she thought wonderingly. How deep did it go? she asked herself for the thousandth time. Deep enough to provide a foundation for love? He claimed to be willing to give up everything for her, and she had never in her life met a man who would have done that. It was growing incredibly difficult to sort out her own feelings where Josh Corbett was concerned. She was going to have to admit to herself, however, that he touched her on more levels, aroused more emotions in her than any other man she'd known. Was she on the verge of falling in love with the man? Or, Lord help her, was she already there?

"I've never been more certain of anything in this world, Reva," he replied with utter conviction, his gaze locking hers in a hypnotic mesh. "Please believe me. I want you so badly it's like a fire in my blood."

Fires, thought Reva with a surge of sadness, had a way of burning themselves out. And then where would she be? With a man like this, she decided in sudden, certain conviction, she would have to be sure of his feelings as well as her own before taking the huge risk of marriage. She had to know the fire in his blood would not flame out when he'd satisfied his obsession with home and wife. But how did any woman assure herself of that kind of guarantee? The divorce courts were full of people who thought they'd been sure the fires wouldn't flame out. In many cases those people had given up a great deal for the other person involved. They wound up rebuilding entire lives!

"Josh," Reva whispered helplessly, but braving the full force of his gaze, "it's such a big step, and one of us would have to give up everything. . . ."

"I've already told you I'm willing to be the one who will give up a job and a past life," he reminded her with soft urgency. "All you have to do is take on the responsibility."

"Of supporting you?" she interrupted, lifting a hand negligently. "That's not the important part, Josh. I could handle the financial end of it."

He looked somewhat astonished at her comment and then his face reflected an unexpected flash of inner laughter. "So generous," he chuckled ruefully. "But I'm not talking about that kind of responsibility, honey. I wouldn't come to you without a decent dowry! I'm talking about the responsibility of making room in your home for me. Of accepting me as the only man in your life. Of sharing your meals and your bed and your Sunday newspaper with me. Do you understand, Reva?"

"Perhaps," she replied a little unsteadily, reaching carefully for the blouse he had flung to the side earlier, "perhaps you'll grow tired of those things after a time." She didn't look at him now as she pulled the garment on, partially concealing her nudity.

"I know what I want, Reva."

"Do you?" She lifted her head again and found him watching her with a wariness that hurt for some obscure reason. She was the one who ought to be wary! "I wouldn't ask anyone to give up another life for the sake of a . . . a temporary obsession or desire, but . . ."

"Damn it, Reva! How many times do I have to tell you . . . !" he began in a fierce growl, only to halt bewilderedly as she held up a hand to silence him.

"But," Reva heard herself say and wondered at her own words, "I believe you think this is what you want and"—she hesitated, searching for the right words and finding only the bald ones—"and I would be an obvious liar if I said I wasn't attracted to you." He looked as if he were about to interrupt her at the small confession and then thought better of it. She saw the way his hard mouth firmed. "I can't think of another man from whom I would have tolerated a fraction of what I've tolerated from you!" she concluded with a small rush of wry honesty.

"Perhaps you're finding out that desire is a stronger force than you once believed it could be," he suggested in what sounded to Reva like a very careful tone of voice.

Or perhaps, Reva told herself silently, I'm finding out that what I feel for you isn't desire at all but something much stronger. Something strong enough to make her more reckless than she had been in a long, long time.

"What are you getting at, Reva?" Josh finally asked, still lying on his back, watching her as she sat up beside him and held the edges of the blouse closed with a faintly trembling hand.

"I was about to suggest," she said with forced calm,

"that we find out how strong your . . . your desire for a home and for me really is without risking everything for it." She swallowed tightly, almost unable to believe her own words but determined now to make the offer. It was the only way, she told herself. The only safe way of finding out how deep his feelings went. The safety, of course, she acknowledged dismally, would be all on his side. But if in the end he changed his mind about his obsession, at least there would be no divorce and she would not have to feel guilty at having been the cause of him ruining his career. Something in Reva shied from wanting to bear that degree of guilt.

"You can't hedge this kind of bet, honey," Josh pointed out quietly, raising himself slowly on one elbow. The dark, heavy brows and narrowed eyes hid much of his expression from her searching gaze.

"We could," she contradicted flatly. "With a sort of trial . . ." Her voice drifted off in a floundering fashion, but she continued to face him.

"A trial marriage? You're offering me an affair? Is that it?"

"You could stay here. Live with me until your leave of absence from your company comes to an end. Maybe you could even get a little more time off. In any event, it would give us both a chance to know each other on a day-to-day basis," Reva explained earnestly. "Then, if, later on, we were sure enough of the relationship to risk marriage, we could talk about which of us should give up the job and . . ."

"Reva," Josh interposed in a very even drawl, "in case you didn't notice, we've already had our affair. I'm looking for marriage, not some milk-and-water association that you'll feel free to break off the next time you get annoyed with me or decide I'm not the perfect escort to your business engagements!"

"You make it sound like I'm offering this to protect myself!" Reva suddenly blazed, hurt that he didn't understand she was taking this approach for his sake as much as for herself.

"Aren't you?" he challenged.

"I'm doing this," she snapped, incensed now, "to give you time to find out if your feelings are more than just an obsession you've developed from living too long in a dangerous and difficult place. At this moment you've convinced yourself you want a home and the security of a marriage, but what guarantee do I have that you won't get the old adventuring urge again and long for your old job and your old friends?"

"As I said," he retorted. "You're just trying to protect yourself!" He moved, tucking his heels into a cross-legged sitting position and reaching out to take hold of her chin with one hand. "But I don't happen to feel like letting you waste that kind of time. I understand that right now you're afraid of the risk involved, but you'll just have to trust me, Reva." He bared his teeth briefly in a wolfish sort of smile. "Will that be so hard to do? After all, you've trusted me before with your life."

"That was different!" Reva tried to pull free of his grasp, but his fingers only tightened in idle warning.

"The difference exists in your head," he groaned. "You've managed to twist what is really a very simple situation into something amazingly complex. What's needed, I think, is a catalyst to help you come to your senses and see things as they are!" He extended his other hand and pulled her off balance and onto his lap where he held her firmly.

"Josh," Reva said with great dignity, even though she

was in a less than dignified position. "Sex is not going to be the magic catalyst that will make me see everything your way!" She lay unresisting in his hold, her head on his bare shoulder.

"Don't you think I've already learned that the hard way?" he mocked, lowering his head to brush her forehead with his lips in a delicate caress. His hand slipped inside her blouse, stroking the warm skin of her waist.

"Then . . . then what's this all about?" she demanded, trying to inject some haughtiness into her words. "You've implied you don't want an affair . . . !"

"I don't," he agreed, dropping another butterflylike kiss on her eyelids. "But a man can get desperate. I'm willing to take what I can get until you give me everything I want." He moved the hand on her stomach upward until it cupped the small weight of her breast, his thumb deliberately teasing at the nipple.

"I fail to see any difference between your attitude and an affair!"

"The difference," he grinned just before he kissed her full on the mouth, "is in my head!" His lips gently but firmly took hers captive for a moment.

"You're making fun of me!" she hissed when she could.

"No, honey, I'm making love to you. There's a difference."

"Only in your head!" Reva shot back, goaded.

He laughed, a deep, surprisingly happy sound.

"Josh, tell me what's going on," she begged, gazing up into the hard face above her. "Are you going to accept my offer of an affair after all?"

"No, sweetheart, I'm not," he grinned cheerfully, but his hand was still possessively shaping her breast and she could sense her own response.

"Then what are you trying to do?"

165

"I've told you, I'll take what I can get until you give me everything," he told her, abandoning his hold on her breast to seek out the softness of her inner thigh.

"But you're not going to call it an affair?" she bit out, feeling a tremor course through her. What new game was he playing? Reva was certain she was being manipulated again, but she couldn't understand how. Damn the man! Never had she been more confused and exasperated by a man in her life!

"Not the sort you implied," he stated. "Because I'm not going to move in with you. I'll just slip across the hall periodically and seduce you," he went on outrageously.

"The hell you will!" Reva abruptly fought free of his hold. He didn't try to stop her as she wriggled off his lap and put distance between them on the carpet. She glared furiously. "I won't be a . . . a casual one-night stand for you, Josh Corbett. If you think I'm going to be available any time you happen to feel like seducing me, you can think again!"

"I thought that's what you were offering," he noted dryly, lion eyes appearing to shimmer slightly as they swept over her disheveled figure.

"I was offering you a sort of trial marriage!" she snapped, annoyed.

"But I'm only interested in the real thing."

"Well, I'm certainly not going to allow you to treat me as a casual fling!"

"There would be nothing casual about it," he retorted meaningfully.

"Josh, you're up to something, I can sense it!" Reva accused belligerently.

"I'm only trying to point out the huge gulf between marriage and nonmarriage, honey," he told her soothingly. "I don't want an in-between ground with you, but if that's what you're offering, I can't turn it down. I won't, however, move in with you until I know for certain you're going to marry me. I'm not going to make things that easy for you!"

"You're twisting this all around, making it sound as if I've got to choose between taking the risk of marriage or seeing you when you feel like seducing me! That's ridiculous!" she stormed, leaping to her feet and grabbing her skirt to hold in front of her. "Furthermore, it won't work because I'm not going to be forced into that kind of decision!" Feeling foolish in her near-naked state, Reva pulled on the skirt and began rebuttoning the blouse.

Josh got lazily to his feet and stood in front of her with a vague, undefined air of gentle menace. "How," he asked coolly, "are you going to avoid the choice?"

Reva lifted her head proudly. "I won't sleep with you on a casual basis and I won't marry you until I'm sure there's something more involved between us than desire and your obsession with having a home, any home! I should be able to survive the next couple of weeks until it's time for you to return to Houston, don't you think?"

"You've already slept with me on what could only be described as a 'casual basis' according to your definition," Josh ground out harshly, honey eyes darkening perceptibly as he watched her taut features. He stood with his hands on his hips, his naked chest a direct affront to Reva's desire to diminish the sexual tension in the room by reclothing herself.

She whitened at the bluntness of his words and fell back a step. "That's not true!"

"What else would you call it?" he grated. "You've slept with me without intending to marry me. What could be more casual than that?"

"Josh, please!"

167

"I, however, have never made love to you without having strictly honorable intentions," he mocked roughly. "And when I make love to you in the future I will continue to do so with the idea of eventually marrying you. But I'm not going to move in and participate in a trial marriage. You're not going to have everything your own way, Reva Waring!" With that, Josh turned to retrieve his shirt, shrugging into it without buttoning it. Without a word he headed for the door, nearly treading on Xavier's tail as he did so. Xavier moved discreetly aside, swiveling his feline head to watch the human leave.

He wasn't the only one viewing the sight, and when the door closed behind Josh, Reva waited tensely for the sound of her neighbor's door being opened. The sound didn't come. After a moment she dared to cross the carpet and open her door a crack. Josh was not in the hallway but the elevator was just sliding shut. He was going out into the night alone.

Reva waited a long time by the front window, gazing down at the sidewalk eighteen floors below, hoping to see Josh returning from wherever he had gone. In the end she gave up and dragged herself slowly off to bed. Never had she felt so depressed and so indecisive. What was she going to do? Battle out the nearly intolerable situation until the time came for Josh to leave for Houston? Would he go back to Texas early if he failed to convince Reva to marry him?

Listlessly, Reva turned in her bed to stroke Xavier in a way that was probably more soothing for her than for him. "What am I going to do, cat? I have the most absurd feeling he's going to win in the end. Not because his will is any stronger than mine, but because I think I'm in love with him. Xavier! He doesn't like the same music or the same books and he's every bit as rough in getting what he

168

wants as I remembered from four months ago! Just look at that stupid trick he pulled on Bruce tonight. And what did I do? I let him serve dinner to his guests and afterward nearly let him make love to me! I must be in love with him to tolerate that sort of behavior! I think I'm going to wind up married to the man, Xavier, but how can I risk that until I know he loves me? Until I know for sure I'm more than a fixation?"

Reva didn't go to sleep until, an endless time later, she finally heard the faint click of Sandy and Tom's door being opened and closed. Josh was safely home. With a sigh she closed her eyes and slept. When the first fringes of the nightmare teased her subconscious mind Reva came awake in a hurry, angry and, as usual, frightened. But this time she determined to handle it by herself, just as she had in the past. And, sliding a little closer to Xavier, she was successful.

Reva left early for the office next morning. There was something orderly and logical about her surroundings at work which she felt instinctively would enable her to think more clearly. She needed to make the decision about marriage to Josh Corbett and she wanted to do it with every bit of her intelligence operating at full capacity. There was a great deal to consider, she told herself as she poured a cup of coffee. Simply coming to the momentous conclusion that she was in love wasn't enough.

Or was it? Wandering from desk to window and back again with the cup in her hand, Reva went over and over the matter, but always logic seemed to drown under the weight of emotion. A little more time, she thought painfully, a little more time to find out how deep Josh's emotions ran. That was what was called for.

She wanted to be sure. She mustn't make the same mistake she had made at twenty-five, she told herself again

169

and again at odd moments during the day. It was true that Josh had turned the tables, placing her in the position of being the one doing the asking, but that didn't make things any easier, Reva discovered.

If anything, she thought late in the afternoon, the responsibility was a heavier weight to bear than anger would have been. The anger she would have felt if she'd been forced to think about giving up her own job wouldn't have carried with it this load of guilt at depriving another individual of such an important part of his life. Josh thought this was what he wanted but what would happen in a few months if he wasn't successful in finding a new position in Portland? Could she weather the storm of his growing frustration and depression? Would her love alone be enough to hold them together during that trying period? If he wasn't in love with her by then, it would be no strange thing if she returned home one day to find him gone.

Reva bit her lip, her thoughts breaking off abruptly as the intercom on her desk buzzed.

"Yes, Anne?" she said automatically, pushing the button on the small instrument.

"A Miss Kemp to see you, Miss Waring." Since Anne always called her boss by her first name except when she was trying to warn her of potential difficulty, Reva went on the alert. Whoever Miss Kemp was, Anne didn't care for her.

"Thank you, Anne. Send her in."

A moment later the door opened and Anne ushered in a strikingly attractive woman who appeared at first glance to be near Reva's own age. One look at her and Reva knew she was meeting someone on her own level of competence and success. A sister businesswoman.

"Elaine Kemp," the other woman said coolly, flicking

dark, almost exotic eyes over Reva as if assessing an opponent. "We've never met. I'm here to see you on a matter of business, however." There was a slight Texas accent.

"Won't you sit down, Miss Kemp?" Reva said politely, as the secretary closed the door. She let her own gaze wander briefly over her visitor, taking in the short, stylishly sassy black hair, the trim figure dressed in a suit that undoubtedly carried a designer's name under the collar, and the real silk of the blue blouse. Anne was right, Reva thought, slightly amused. There was an almost intimidating look about Elaine Kemp. Reva wondered idly if she herself presented that appearance to strangers, and then dismissed the thought. A bit of subtle intimidation was sometimes necessary in business.

"Thank you," Elaine Kemp said, sinking gracefully into the indicated chair. "I'll come right to the point. My business with you is somewhat of a personal nature. It regards a mutual acquaintance. Josh Corbett."

Reva limited her reaction to a slightly raised eyebrow. "I rather gathered that when I heard the southern accent. We don't get that many Texans in Portland. Please go on." Reva disregarded her small lie. She sensed instinctively it was crucial not to let Elaine Kemp somehow gain the upper hand in their association, and making her think she'd guessed the purpose of the visit was a small way of letting the other woman know she wasn't precisely stunned. Later, Reva promised, she would admit to herself just how stunned she really was. Elaine Kemp was the last thing in the world she had expected this afternoon. What did this beautiful, sophisticated woman have to do with Josh?

"You know where Josh is?" Elaine inquired coolly, opening her small, elegant leather purse and removing a cigarette and lighter.

"Yes, of course I know." Reva waited, watching as Elaine calmly lit the cigarette and exhaled languidly.

"Excellent. His telegram didn't mention his own address, only your work location. I came here as soon as I got off the plane."

"To find out where Josh is?" Reva clarified, debating whether or not to tell the woman. She thought she'd call Josh first and ask him if he wanted to be found.

"That and a few other things," Elaine Kemp chuckled in her throaty voice. "The telegram was characteristically brief, saying only that he was resigning to marry you unless someone from the company could change his mind for him. I was sent to do the job."

It took all of Reva's willpower to hide her start of surprise. What had Josh done?

"He's handed in his resignation, Miss Kemp?" She couldn't believe it!

"With the qualifier I just mentioned. I have every confidence, Miss Waring, that I shall find a lure which will succeed in making Josh change his mind. I have instructions to inform him his salary is quite open to negotiation, as are his benefits. He can very nearly name his own price."

"His firm must want him back very badly," Reva observed, stalling for a little time while she tried to sort through the implications of this latest development.

"It does. He's one of the few people on the staff who would be asked to reconsider his decision. We have great hopes, naturally, that he will reconsider. After all, he invited us to try and change his mind." Elaine smiled with deep challenge. "Usually when Josh makes a decision that's the end of the matter. He leaves no loopholes or dangling ends."

"But this time he did and you're wondering how much

172

of a dangling end I am," Reva nodded calmly. What new game was Josh Corbett playing?

"Exactly."

"Tell me, Miss Kemp, what does Josh do for your company? He told me he was some sort of troubleshooter."

"That's not his official title," Elaine said in amusement, tapping her cigarette against the ashtray Reva kept for visitors. "But it's an apt description of his work. I don't hesitate to tell you, Reva, that Josh's abilities and skills are rather unique. We would have a great deal of trouble trying to replace him. It's highly doubtful we could turn up anyone else with his curious combination of abilities in anything under a year or two. If then!"

"His contacts in South America are so valuable to your firm?" Reva questioned intently.

"Among other things," Elaine nodded. "A few months ago, for example, he single-handedly convinced the important people of one government down there to resist the temptation of nationalizing our company's holdings and seizing its assets in the country. As the government was involved in putting down a small but rather violent revolution at the time, it was a major accomplishment. The action alone justified his salary for the next ten years!"

"You speak very highly of him," Reva smiled lazily. "How long has Josh been doing this sort of thing?"

"As long as I've been with the firm, which is about five years. He was on board a couple years before that, I believe. Prior to his experience with us I'm not exactly sure what he did for a living. There are always rumors about a man like Josh," Elaine shrugged lightly. "Some say he worked for intelligence, some say he operated a one-man cargo plane for hire in South America, flying places others wouldn't. No one knows the full truth but that's all right, don't you think? It adds a rather nice touch of mystery and excitement, as I'm sure you've discovered."

"And you, Miss Kemp?" Reva murmured, letting only a mild chill enter her voice. "Do you also enjoy the touch of mystery and excitement?"

"Oh, yes," Elaine drawled easily. "Why do you think I was the one the boss sent to try and change Josh's mind?" The dark eyes flashed in amusement. "Josh and I were becoming very, um, how shall I phrase it? *involved* with each other shortly before this last jaunt to South America. I have no doubt I can convince him to take up where he left off four months ago."

"Any idea why he didn't rush right back to you after his work was over?" Reva inquired with great dryness. She'd seen the way Elaine Kemp's dark eyes had flickered with excitement as she talked of Josh and his vague past. Reva didn't like the impression she was getting that Josh's main attraction for this woman lay in the implied danger which touched his past and his present.

"It is not unnatural for a man like Josh Corbett to find himself a woman to amuse him as soon as he returns from an assignment. His relationship with me extends to more important levels. He doesn't use me in that way, you understand. When he comes to me it's for something much more important than a brief, relaxing fling. I assume he encountered you somewhere en route on his way out of South America. Possibly on the plane. It's happened before. The only thing different about this time is that he's using you to get a little more money and probably more vacation time from the company. I'm here to tell him he can have it."

"You think he's using me to threaten your firm?" Reva grated gently, shocked to discover she hadn't even consid-

174

ered that possibility. Was Josh involving her in some sort of plot to extract a higher salary? What *was* he up to? she wondered despairingly.

"Let's just say you were convenient," Elaine smiled with cold superiority. "Don't take it personally, Reva, I'm sure Josh is enjoying his brief stay in Portland, as he enjoyed his last brief stay in San Diego. It was an airline stewardess that time, I think. But he always comes back when he's through with his R and R."

"His work is always as dangerous and as difficult as this business four months ago?" Reva frowned, choosing to ignore Elaine's remark about the stewardess. She found herself much more concerned about the kind of life Josh was leading.

"He thrives on it," Elaine chuckled. "As long as I can remember, Josh has been the one sent when things got difficult. A multinational company has a tough time in today's world, Reva, as I'm sure you can imagine. It needs many of the same things a government needs; a diplomatic arm, an intelligence arm, and someone who can operate in shifting waters which, as in the case of South America or the Middle East, can turn violent."

"And that's what Josh has been doing for your firm for the past few years," Reva said slowly, consideringly. "That doesn't sound like it gives him much of a home life."

"Men like Josh don't have any interest in a 'home life,' " Elaine laughed, squashing her cigarette. "And let's be honest with each other, Reva Waring, would either of us be particularly interested in him if he were to suddenly become the homebody, nine-to-five type? I doubt it!"

CHAPTER NINE

Reva stared in cool silence at the sleek woman sitting opposite. "You seem very sure of your knowledge of Josh," she finally said without inflexion. If Josh truly wanted a real home he'd never find it working for his present employer, Reva thought sadly. He'd been cast as an adventuring troubleshooter and that's the role he'd be expected to continue playing. How did a man break out of that kind of mold? Idly she toyed with the pencil beside the coffee cup.

"I am. I've known him well for almost a year, and I knew about him from the first day I was hired. Everyone knows about Josh," Elaine purred with an air of superiority. For the first time Reva began to wonder just how much everyone knew about Josh Corbett.

"What if he means what he says?" Reva finally asked slowly, thoughtfully. "What if he seriously is considering marriage?"

"If you knew him better, you'd know that when Josh seriously considers doing something he doesn't invite others to talk him out of it!" Elaine retorted. "No, it's very obvious he's using you to get the boss to come through with better compensation. He should have known he didn't have to go to these lengths!"

"You don't consider me much of a threat, is that it?"

Reva smiled, wondering if her own blue-green eyes had gone as cold as Elaine Kemp's dark ones.

"I'm afraid not," the other woman assured her. "I'm here only because Josh gave me no alternative than to come to you for his current address. Would you mind very much providing it? I'm wasting time. Is he staying with you?" Elaine didn't seem particularly worried about that possibility, merely somewhat resigned.

"Not exactly," Reva told her slowly, and reached for the phone. Elaine watched with barely concealed excitement as she dialed her neighbor's number. She's enjoying this, Reva abruptly realized. Elaine Kemp was getting a kick out of playing Josh's latest game. Reva shivered invisibly as the phone rang on the other end.

"Hello?" It was Tom's voice, sounding quite cheerful.

"Tom? This is Reva. Is Josh around?"

"Hang on a second and I'll get him. Keep him on the line a few minutes, will you? It will give me time to rig the chess game. I haven't won yet!"

Reva blinked, remembering the series of small games she had played with Josh the day he'd pretended to be ill. Josh had lost at every single play. She sighed silently, sure now that the losing had been deliberate. Wheels within wheels. Who could figure out what Josh was plotting next? The only way any of it made sense was if he was telling the truth. That he wanted to marry and settle down.

"Reva?" It was Josh, sounding mildly amused. "What did you have for lunch today?" He didn't seem at all upset about the previous night's parting.

The unexpected inquiry brought a frown to Reva's carefully composed features.

"An apple," she answered obediently, without thinking. "Josh, I'm calling to tell you that . . ."

"Tom and I sent out for a pizza," he went on with

relish, "which we shared with Xavier." Where had he gone last night? she wondered again.

"Tom and you and Xavier are all going to get fat if you keep that up," Reva retorted. "Josh, listen to me, there's someone . . ."

"You're just jealous."

"Probably," Reva agreed on a groan. "Josh, there's someone here in my office asking for you," she managed in a rush before he could say anything else.

"Let me guess. Texas accent?" he asked chattily, not sounding at all concerned.

"Yes, as a matter of fact." Reva glanced across her desk at Elaine, who was listening intently to every word.

"Male or female?"

"Josh, this is hardly a guessing game," Reva grumbled. "I take it you were expecting someone?"

"Sure. How do you think she got your address? It is a she, isn't it? Crawford would probably send someone like Elaine Kemp," Josh deduced with such ease that Reva was forced to conclude he'd known all along who was in the office.

"Would you like to speak to her? She's asking for your present address," Reva told him tightly, realizing she didn't care one bit for being in the middle of this little exercise.

"Not particularly." Reva could almost see the shrug. "Bring her home if you think I should see her." There was a significant pause. "I'll leave it entirely in your hands, honey." The phone went dead as Josh hung up, leaving Reva with an itch to throttle him again for having put her in her present position.

Elaine's dark eyes were speculative as she lit another cigarette and watched Reva replace the receiver. "He's going to go on playing hide-and-seek?" she drawled lightly.

"No," said Reva with sudden decision. Damned if she would let herself be used this way! "He'll see you if you want to go to that address." She scrawled Tom and Sandy's address on a slip of paper with a flourish. She didn't know for certain what Josh was up to this time, but she was determined not to play until she knew all aspects of the game. That man had manipulated her enough in the past few days!

"Thanks," Elaine said briefly, reaching for the paper and getting to her feet. "I'll take a cab. This is a downtown address, isn't it?"

"That's right," Reva agreed distantly, not bothering to mention that she herself was on her way home and could easily give the other woman a ride. "Good-bye, Miss Kemp."

"Aren't you going to wish me luck in convincing Josh to return to Texas?" Elaine laughed chidingly as she headed for the door.

"Luck," Reva smiled serenely, "will have nothing to do with it. Josh makes his own rules as he goes along."

And, as her own perverse luck would have it, Reva decided some time later, as she finally parked her car in her garage and took the elevator up to the eighteenth floor, she hadn't been able to get to the apartment ahead of the other woman. Something unexpected had arisen at the office and it had taken her an extra half hour to sort out the matter. She had hoped to be safely established behind her own locked door when Elaine Kemp came knocking on her neighbor's door! The small traffic jam on the bridge she had chosen delayed her still further and Reva finally thrust her key in the lock a full hour beyond her normal arrival time.

"There you are, Reva," Sandy's cheerful voice caught her just as Reva was about to step into the privacy of her own apartment. "You're just in time to help us make the decision."

Reva turned, startled, to glance at Sandy, who was grinning at her from the apartment doorway. "What decision?" she asked carefully, not wanting to have a run-in with Josh until she'd settled a few things in her own mind. She might be in love with the man, she admitted grimly, but that didn't mean she was going to make a complete fool of herself.

"Josh is trying to choose a tie for this evening. He certainly travels with a large collection of them, doesn't he?" Sandy stepped back invitingly. "Do come in before Tom has the final say."

"That's all right, Sandy, I was going to make myself a light dinner and . . ."

"You can do that later. Come on in. This is great fun!" Sandy extended a hand out into the corridor and grasped Reva's arm, pulling her into the hall. Gritting her teeth, Reva allowed herself to be reluctantly hauled into her neighbor's living room, where Josh was standing in front of an ornate mirror, loosening the knot of a particularly colorful example of the necktie maker's art. Tom sat beside him in his wheelchair, holding half a dozen more equally colorful ties.

"Hello, Reva, come to help me decide?" Josh inquired smoothly, catching her eye in the mirror. "Tom thinks red's a good color to wear when negotiating with an employer. Sandy thinks something more conservative would be best. I was all set to wear this one when everyone started getting into the act." He held up a brilliantly splashed design which looked something like a Fourth of July fireworks explosion against a black background.

"You're going out this evening?" Reva said quietly, ignoring the tie after one glance. "With Miss Kemp?"

"She came by about an hour ago. Since you'd obviously given her the address, I figured you must want me to see her." Josh shrugged, reaching for the next tie in Tom's hand.

Tom smiled blandly at Reva. "Personally, with Elaine's black hair and dark eyes, I think the red one's the best, don't you? Very striking."

"Nonsense," Sandy broke in with great feeling. "It may be a date, but we must keep in mind that Miss Kemp is representing Josh's firm. This is also a business meeting and therefore calls for something conservative. Tom, you may have to loan Josh one of yours," she added thoughtfully, frowning.

"Perhaps," Josh said very quietly, the lion eyes still holding Reva's in the mirror, "All this is unnecessary. Perhaps Reva would rather I didn't go out this evening after all."

There was a tense and significant pause as Sandy and Tom turned to look at Reva with great expectancy. Reva felt the emotions which had been churning in her all day resolve into anger. Josh Corbett was trying to force her hand, she realized bleakly. Did he really think she was such a poor opponent that he could manipulate her this way? Or was he playing the game Elaine Kemp seemed to feel he was? In any event, Reva thought painfully, she would not be drawn into this ridiculous business. Josh could make his own decision about quitting his job! And if he did quit, she wouldn't have to face the guilt.

"I think," she said softly, evenly, "that one should examine all sides of a situation before coming to a decision. It's only good business to hear what Miss Kemp has to offer."

"Will I be receiving a counteroffer?" Josh mused with apparent academic interest only.

"Miss Kemp's offer might be difficult to counter," Reva returned coolly. "I understand she's been given carte blanche."

"Still," Josh went on, slowly knotting another tie, "there may be some things Elaine can't offer."

"Things you really want?" Reva heard herself say a little breathlessly, unaware of Sandy and Tom listening to the conversation intently.

"Yes . . ." Josh's words were cut off as the doorbell rang.

"That will be Elaine," he said calmly, finishing the knot on his tie and standing away from the mirror to reach for his jacket.

"She's picking you up?" Reva asked, astonished and appalled that time had just run out.

"Naturally," Josh told her, shrugging into his jacket, the lion eyes meshing with Reva's wide blue-green ones. "She's the one bidding for me, why shouldn't she be the one who does the running around?"

"The liberated male," Tom put in admiringly.

"Don't get any ideas," Sandy told him ferociously.

"What . . . what time do you expect her to bring you back?" Reva couldn't believe she'd asked such a revealing and ridiculous question. She'd have given anything to have the words unsaid, even though they were similar to the words Josh had said when she'd gone out with Bruce.

"Why don't you wait up for me and find out?" Josh murmured as Sandy hurried to the door and opened it.

"You'd like that, wouldn't you?" Reva grumbled, stepping aside. "Two women 'bidding' for you!"

"I'm quite prepared to forego listening to the company's best offer tonight and hear yours instead," he told her bluntly, ignoring the vision of dark, exotic loveliness

183

which was stepping into the hall. "All you have to do is ask me to stay home tonight, Reva."

"You're trying to force me into making the decision!" she accused wretchedly, horribly conscious of Elaine waiting at the door.

"I'm trying to make you understand your own feelings about stray alley cats," he retorted, hard mouth quirking wryly. "Do you really want to send me back out into the cold?"

"Ready, Josh?" Elaine's soft, southern accent floated toward him and he glanced around at her.

"I guess so," he replied, slanting a last, challenging look at Reva, who stood mute, her hands clenched together so tightly the knuckles had gone white. "Good night, Reva." He turned and walked toward Elaine, who smiled with knowing victory as she took his arm. The sleek black dress she wore emphasized her mysterious air and sophisticated beauty. Small diamonds glimmered in her ears and the short black hair was a shining cap that framed beautifully made-up eyes to perfection. Reva wanted to go for the other woman's throat and the power of her own feelings stunned her so that she swayed slightly as the other two disappeared out the door without a backward glance.

"Well," Tom sighed ruefully, looking at the ties remaining in his hand, "he didn't wear the red one after all."

"I think he settled on that fireworks thing," Sandy nodded. "The one he picked out first. So much for the conservative voice in the crowd."

"He wore what he wanted to wear," Reva sighed, moving slowly toward the door. "He usually does things his own way. Good night, you two. I'll see you later."

Back in her own apartment Reva changed into her warmest, fluffiest housecoat, tied her hair into a careless knot, and fed a complaining Xavier. When the cat was at

184

last quietly eating in his usual efficient style, Reva glanced morosely into her refrigerator. There was nothing of interest, not even a slice of leftover pizza, she thought wryly. She poured herself a glass of wine, cut a slice of cheese, and wandered dispiritedly out into the living room to eat in front of the evening news on television.

"What do you suppose he's doing now?" she asked Xavier a few minutes later as the cat emerged from the kitchen, licking his whiskers in satisfaction. At the sound of her voice he ambled forward and leaped lightly into her lap, nosing at the cheese. "Get away from there," she ordered. "You already had your dinner." Out of self-defense she ate the cheese quickly.

"I wonder if they're going to that restaurant down by the river where Josh took me the other night," she remarked to the cat. "It's about the only place Josh knows in town." The thought was depressing in the extreme.

Reva tried to put the image of Josh pouring wine into Elaine's glass out of her mind and concentrate on the latest flare-up in the Middle East. The sort of flare-up Josh was likely to get caught in, came an unbidden thought. How much longer was he going to risk his neck for his employer?

But if he wanted out as badly as he seemed to imply, why didn't he go ahead and make the break? Why was he trying to force Reva to guarantee him a home before he actually quit his job? Perhaps she, Reva, wasn't all that important after all. Perhaps she was only being used to further his interest at the company. It was even possible, Reva told herself, that Josh did want out of the trouble-shooting role but didn't want to leave the firm. Perhaps, she acknowledged, her tongue touching her lower lip thoughtfully, Josh's demands to the firm would have nothing to do with money, but with a change in assignment.

But Elaine Kemp had made it clear Josh's chief value to the company lay in his contacts abroad. Even if he got himself a less adventuring sort of assignment, he would still be traveling a great deal. No home life at all, Reva told herself, taking another sip of wine.

"A high-paid alley cat, Xavier, that's what he'll be." Reva got up and poured herself another glass of wine, glancing idly at her watch. "A high-paid alley cat doomed to wander the alleys of South America forever." The theatrical thought forced Reva to smile wanly at herself. Then she remembered Elaine Kemp and sighed, curling back onto the red sofa. The gleam of excitement in the other woman's eyes tonight had been positively revolting. Elaine loved the touch of danger and intrigue about Josh Corbett. As the dark-haired woman had said, remove it and he wouldn't be nearly so interesting to her. Reva's mouth tightened in disgust.

Josh could do better than Elaine Kemp. He needed someone who would love him for himself. The only thing that could be said about her own emotions toward Josh Corbett, Reva concluded, was that she didn't love him for his exotic past. Instead, she wanted to protect him from that. She might as well face it. She wanted to give him a home and love. Josh hadn't asked for love, she reminded herself sadly. But he had asked for a home and for her.

Around midnight Reva dozed gently over the mystery novel in her lap. She awoke with a small start when Xavier moved, stretching, yawning, and then hopping down off the red sofa to pad silently toward the front door. Reva stared vaguely after him and then heard the sound of hushed voices. Josh and Elaine had returned.

Stirring, Reva untucked her legs and padded after Xavier, not precisely certain what she was going to do but feeling an overpowering urge to do something. The game

186

had gone on long enough. She had decided that much, if nothing else, this evening.

Not bothering to check her somewhat sleepy appearance in the mirror, Reva halted in front of the door, her hand on the knob. Listening intently she could barely make out the throaty words of Elaine Kemp.

"You'll think about our offer?" There was a meaningful pause. "My offer?"

"I'll think about it," Josh promised in a neutral tone that told Reva absolutely nothing about what he was thinking. "You'd better hurry. The cab is waiting downstairs."

Reva blinked in mild surprise. Josh wasn't even going to see his date home? Apparently he'd meant it when he said Elaine could do the running around. Of course the other woman would be safe enough going in a cab straight to her hotel, but still . . . ! Josh was not always the perfect gentleman, Reva told herself. But, then, she already knew that, didn't she? She'd had more than one lesson on the subject.

"You're sure you won't change your mind and come back to the hotel with me?" Elaine murmured invitingly.

"Not tonight, Elaine," Josh returned quietly. "Perhaps another time."

"When you return to Houston?"

"If I return to Houston," he corrected mildly.

Reva waited no longer. She flung open the door and Xavier trotted out into the hall to greet Josh. "Does that mean," she began very carefully, knowing her whole future was being determined, "that you're still open to counteroffers?"

Head high, her regal air not diminished by the housecoat and slightly askew topknot, Reva met Josh's eyes as he and Elaine turned to look at her. She saw the honey-colored flames leap to life in the golden-brown gaze as Josh took in the picture she made standing in the doorway.

"Yes," he told her softly, deliberately. "I'm still very much open to another offer. Are you prepared to make one?" He waited, his outwardly cool façade not quite concealing the wariness and watchfulness in his hard, lean frame. Reva saw it and was touched. He was like Xavier, trying to be so cool and manipulative and underneath wanting something so bad he couldn't quite hide it.

"Would you care to come inside and listen to my proposal?" Reva whispered. She pushed the door open a little wider and waited. Her eyes were fastened almost painfully on Josh's face and she ignored Elaine's impatient little movement.

"What's going on here, Josh?" Elaine demanded. "Why is this woman always hanging around? What's she got to do with you, anyway?"

"You've got it all wrong, Elaine," Josh said distantly, disengaging his arm from the dark-haired woman's hold. "It's not Reva who's hanging around me; I'm the one hanging around Reva. Like a stray cat. Good night, Elaine. Tell Crawford I've made up my mind. I am declining his very generous offers. My resignation is final." Without glancing again at the shocked and incredulous face of his acquaintance from Texas, Josh stepped forward, Xavier at his heels. Reva fell back into the hall as they walked into the apartment, closing the door firmly behind themselves.

Outside the door Reva heard Elaine's unstifled oath and then, a moment later, the sound of the elevator announcing its arrival.

"She's gone," Reva said gently, not taking her eyes off Josh, who stood about two feet away.

188

"It doesn't matter."

"You're very sure this is what you want?" she whispered.

"You're offering me marriage?" he verified cautiously, one brow lifting with unconscious intimidation.

Reva took a deep breath. "Yes." The tension vibrated between them.

"Then it's what I want." He took a step forward and paused, not touching her. "It's what I've wanted all along. Why do you think I sent the telegram to Crawford in the first place?"

"You knew he'd send Elaine?"

"It was a safe bet. Once you saw her I was fairly certain you'd be induced to save me from her clutches." There was the hint of a satisfied, if still cautious smile in the lion eyes.

"It wasn't just her, Josh, it was that whole job. She described your work to me and implied it's what you'd be doing the rest of your career. No home life at all . . ." Reva's voice trailed off a little uncertainly as she looked earnestly up into his face. She couldn't bring herself to say the rest. Not yet. The moment was too fragile, too delicate to be blurting out her love. A love he had never included in his list of demands.

"And you decided to take me away from all that?" he murmured in soft mockery. But the honey eyes were warm. "Make an honest man out of me?"

"If that's what you want," she nodded, her mouth suddenly very dry.

"What do you want, Reva?" he surprised her by asking almost tersely.

"I want you to leave that awful job down in Texas, move to Portland, and marry me," she told him starkly. And I want you to learn to love me, she added silently.

189

"Thank you. I accept." With a low groan, he moved, taking the last step that brought him against her and taking her into his arms.

Reva felt herself being gently and inexorably crushed into the fabric of his jacket and her arms wrapped around his waist as she surrendered to the embrace. For a long time he made no effort to kiss her, seeming content to hold her tightly against him, inhaling the scent of her hair. She could feel the shudder that went through him after a moment and knew it reflected the hunger and male need that simmered just under the surface. A hunger and need that weren't only sexual in nature. Reva sensed the feelings went much deeper than that and sighed, relaxing still further against him. She would build on those needs and teach this man to love.

"Reva?" His voice was low and husky in her ear.

"Yes, Josh?" Her head was still buried in his jacket.

"Reva, honey, I want you so badly."

"Yes, Josh."

She felt his lips on the nape of her neck and his large hands shifted to cup her hips, pulling her more closely, intimately against him. She was aware of the tremors coursing through both of them and she slid her hands up under his jacket, reveling in the warmth of his body.

"I'll take good care of you, sweetheart," he murmured deeply, arching her back against his arm so that his lips could find the hollow of her shoulder, which was slightly exposed by the collar of her housecoat.

"You've always taken good care of me," she half-smiled, feeling a rush of warmth and longing. "And I'll do my best to look after you, too."

He chuckled softly. "How can we lose?" he growled, sweeping her into his arms and heading for the bedroom. Once there he set her carefully on her feet, turned back the

190

covers, and began to remove the housecoat. The hungry lion eyes never left her face as he slowly undid the belt at her waist.

"I was hoping you'd wait up for me," he smiled, slipping his hands into the opening of the garment.

"Did you have any doubts?" she demanded ruefully, shaking her head as she surveyed the look of male pleasure in his face. She lifted her hands to his shoulders and smiled again.

"A few," he confessed. "I wasn't sure how quickly the catalyst of Elaine would work." Her housecoat slid to the floor at her feet and Josh stood drinking in the sight of her slenderness as he began to loosen the flashy tie. The fine, satiny material of Reva's nightgown outlined the gentle curve of her small breasts and the shape of her hip to perfection.

"But you were sure that ultimately it would work?" she teased, sliding the jacket gently off his shoulders.

He reached out and removed her glasses, smiling down into the blue-green eyes. "If it hadn't I would have tried something else. I don't give up that easily!"

With increasing urgency and mounting desire, Josh removed the rest of his clothes, tossing them into an uncaring heap on the floor. He stood for a moment before Reva, uncompromisingly male and unconsciously arrogant in his masculinity. But Reva knew of the gentleness in him and when he had stripped the nightgown from her she went into his arms with total assurance and trust.

"I don't think," he grated hoarsely as he picked her up and set her on the bed, "that I can ever get enough of you, little Reva." His face was a strange mixture of desire, restraint, and vulnerability as he followed her down onto the bed and pulled her on top of him.

Reva smiled down into his eyes, her hair coming loose

to sweep against his chest as he drove his fingers possessively through the knot of it. With her fingers she began
kneading the broad shoulders, exploring the strength of
him and enjoying the sensation of having him, for once,
at her mercy. It was an illusion, she knew, one that would
change as soon as he tired of the love game and drew her
underneath him for the final claiming.

But in the meantime, Reva thought, covering his chest
with kisses and using her fingers to tease and arouse, in the
meantime she was free to make love to him as she wished.

She heard his groans and felt the trembling in his hands
as he gently raked the skin of her back down to her thighs.
She shuddered in turn and a soft moan escaped her throat.
The sound seemed to please him, excite him, and a moment later Reva felt herself lifted easily, lightly from her
sprawl atop his chest and settled beside him in the crook
of his arm.

He bent to kiss her, his hands straying over her body,
boldly caressing and striving to bring her to his own level
of desire.

"Reva, my sweet, you can't imagine what it's been like
not knowing when I'd have you permanently in my bed!
Having you so close but not knowing for certain when the
game would be over!" Her ankle was chained beneath one
of his and he used the pressure of his foot to pull her legs
slightly, tantalizingly apart, opening her softness to the
hungry exploration of his hands.

"Is that all it was, Josh?" Reva heard herself say in a
funny, distant voice, even as the fire caught in her loins
and her response leaped to match his. She turned into his
warmth, the male scent of him a summons she could not
deny. "Was it all just a game for you?" Her voice was
muffled against the skin of his shoulder.

"It only became a game, a very unnecessary game," he

192

told her almost grimly, "when I arrived home to find you pretending not to have been expecting me! But I knew, the night you came creeping into my bed, that everything was just as it had been back there in the jungle and that it was only a matter of time before you'd see that."

Reva wanted to say something else, something about loving him and wanting to be loved in return, but she couldn't find the words in that moment as passion mounted. Her body was vibrating in response to his touch and the heavy presence of him so much that she couldn't speak sensibly.

"Oh, Josh!" Her breath came quickly between her teeth and the blue-green eyes slitted against a pleasure that was very nearly a pain, so strong was desire now. She felt his mouth stopping hers, silencing her small cries with sudden sensuous ferocity as he loomed over her, lowering himself into her softness with unrestrained need and power.

Reva felt his weight once more on her and her hands clutched wildly around his neck as he took her, claiming her for his own once again. And once again Reva was completely enthralled by the overwhelming embrace, the undisguised, naked, challenging desire and need in him. She gave herself up to the joy of satisfying the man who held her and greedily took her own satisfaction from him.

When at long last Reva emerged from the cloudy world where Josh had taken her, she moved her head slightly to look at him as he lay beside her on the pillow. His eyes were closed and he held her hand tightly against his chest. She stared at him for a moment, wonderingly, and then the lion eyes opened lazily to smile into hers.

Without a word he lifted the hand he held and kissed her fingertips.

"Mine," he whispered softly, contentedly. "All mine. There's no going back this time, Reva," he told her with

193

absolute authority. "No more sleeping alone for either of us. No more games. No more arguments about the two of us not being right for each other."

"You think all our differences are behind us?" Reva teased, touching the side of his cheek with gentle, questing fingers.

"No, but they're unimportant beside the one salient fact of the matter," he told her with casual promise.

"Which is?" she asked boldly.

"Which is that you belong to me. You have since I brought you out of that jungle four months ago. And now you've accepted me, given me my saucer of milk. You've taken on the responsibility of making a home for me and you can't back out of the deal. Not this time."

There was such will and intent in the gravelly voice that Reva could only stare quietly back at him for a moment, trying to understand the source of his urgency.

Was it that, in spite of his words and possessive actions, Josh was still afraid he couldn't really force her to keep her new stray cat? Was he thinking of all he had abandoned tonight when he'd turned his back on Elaine Kemp, how many risks he was taking? He had, after all, walked out on a way of life he'd known for a long time. A way of life in which he had excelled.

With understanding in her eyes Reva smiled at the man who shared her bed. She knew how she would be feeling if the positions were reversed and it was she who had just given up everything. Oh, yes, she knew very well how she would be feeling. And because she knew it, Reva found herself several times more than sympathetic to the uncertainty she thought she sensed in Josh Corbett.

"You've had enough of living out of suitcases, Josh," she whispered gently. "It's time you had a home of your own. The home you've been wanting. It was a lousy job, even if it did pay well. A lousy job for a man who wants a home. You couldn't have both."

"I know that," he told her with a quirking little smile. "I have no regrets about my choice." But there was still something in his voice.

"You won't feel eventually that it should have been me who resigned?" she asked with a touch of worry.

He chuckled at that. "No. At first I suppose I assumed you'd be coming back to Houston with me. One always thinks first of the woman leaving her world to join her husband's. I had some vague idea of working out a different arrangement with the firm; getting myself a nice desk job in the Houston office. I knew four months ago I wasn't going back to the constant travel and the life I'd been leading. When you asked me if I'd give up my job, hypothetically speaking, of course," he grinned suddenly, "I realized that was the perfect answer. All that remained was to convince you to do the asking!"

"No regrets?"

"No regrets," he assured her.

And Reva snuggled down against him, wondering why her instincts told her he was still hedging his answer.

CHAPTER TEN

"I didn't know you liked to ski," Reva said three mornings later, slanting a glance across the car seat at the man who had only a short time earlier become her husband.

"Relieved to find out we have something in common after all?" Josh grinned, guiding the car along the narrowing mountain road. Snow lay in a thick mantle on the ground and encrusted the trees. It made a lovely picture and Reva was already thinking of hot toddies near a blazing hearth.

"Well, if you're faking your way through this one, it should be interesting to see how you manage!" she teased, watching snowflakes bounce against the windshield. The light shower seemed to be intensifying.

"Sadist," he grumbled good-naturedly, concentrating on the slick road. "You're insisting on a skiing honeymoon just so you can watch me take a fall. But I'm not worried. If I can fake my way through Mozart, I can fake it down a ski slope!"

"Are there any lengths to which you won't go in order to assure yourself a good home?" Reva smiled affectionately, enjoying the close, intimate atmosphere of the car. It seemed so right having Josh beside her like this. She wondered how she had ever imagined going through life without him. If only, she thought hesitantly, she knew for certain what seemed to be riding him at times. It was almost impossible to put a name to, this hint of wariness that she sensed in him. She wondered once more if he was already regretting his decision to walk out on everything he'd known in Houston. Determinedly she put the notion behind her. The past three days had been a whirlwind created by Josh and it had been difficult to find time to even think. She was probably imagining things.

"None," he vowed, flicking a honey glance at her. There was no question of the purposefulness and intent in those eyes, Reva thought. She was crazy to even think he had any other thoughts but settling into the married life. "I'm like Xavier. A one-track mind."

"Speaking of Xavier," she chuckled, "I hope he isn't feeling abandoned."

"Tom and Sandy will take good care of him," Josh shrugged, wide shoulders moving easily under the thick pullover sweater he wore. The sweater was a gift from Reva, who realized he was going to need some additions to his wardrobe if they were to spend the week skiing. "Besides, that cat's got more sense than to want to spend a week in snow!"

"Don't look at me when you say that!" Reva chided humorously. "You were the one who insisted on a honeymoon somewhere that didn't remind you of a hot, steamy jungle!"

"Umm," he muttered noncommittally. "Does it seem to you the snow on the windshield is getting heavier?"

"Yes. I expect that storm they predicted on the radio last night is ahead of schedule. No need to worry. We should be at the lodge in another half hour or so." Reva glanced again at her map and then went on chattily as her thoughts flew back to the small, private wedding that

198

morning. "That was certainly a nice wedding present we had from Tom," she smiled happily.

"The good news from his doctor yesterday? You can say that again. I heard him tell Tom myself that the critical point was past. It's just a matter of time until he's back on his feet again."

"Sandy appreciated you taking Tom to the clinic for that visit. Did you realize she was aware all along what was worrying Tom but didn't want to let him know she knew? That's why she was so grateful for you taking him yesterday. She knew it would be easier for her husband to handle bad news with a man present." Reva sighed, shaking her head. "Thank God that's almost over."

"They should have talked about it openly," Josh announced. "What was the point of trying to protect each other like that? That's what marriage is designed for, to give . . ." Reva could have sworn he nearly stumbled over a word, but he finished smoothly, "support and strength to each other."

"Josh, the great expert on marriage," Reva giggled delightedly. "For someone who has put it off as long as you have, I find your newfound command of the subject most enlightening!"

"I'm not the only one who waited longer than usual," he pointed out kindly.

"Are you saying I was almost over the hill?" she demanded spiritedly.

"It's all right," he told her, "I realize you're probably a little set in your ways, but you'll come around. This matter of wanting to go on using your former name, for example . . ." he began determinedly.

"It's not my *former* name, it's my name. Period," Reva retorted, not particularly worried about the matter. "I've built a career under Reva Waring and I see no reason to change it."

"You will," he grinned. "I'll just keep wearing you down, like water on rock."

"Why?" she asked rather curiously. The name business was something of a game to her. Her career didn't depend on her last name and if Josh really wanted her to change it to his, she would. After all, he'd certainly given up enough for her! But in the meantime the banter over the issue was fun.

"I like the implication of ownership," he shot back with a wicked chuckle. "Reva Corbett makes it sound as if you belong to me. It tells other men to keep their hands off!"

"But if I'm almost beyond my prime anyway, what danger can there be from other men?" she retorted.

"Unfortunately," he sighed grimly, "that danger is never gone."

"Well, I certainly would hate to have to keep patching you up after every fight." Laughter danced in her eyes as Reva remembered the fall Josh had taken when Bruce Tanner had finally been persuaded to swing at him. She wondered if Bruce would ever realize how lucky he'd been.

"That's right. Have a bit of pity for me," he encouraged, negotiating a slippery turn with caution. There was silence for a moment as he concentrated on the driving and then he said very calmly, "I wonder, Mrs. Corbett, if you would mind double-checking that map again. Just to reassure me."

"You're not implying I might have gotten us lost, I hope!" Reva sniffed, shuffling the map and peering carefully at it.

"I wouldn't think of making such an accusation on our wedding day," he responded quite silkily. "But I wonder

if there might be a distant possibility of a temporary diso-
rientation?"

Reva frowned. "I'm very good with maps."

"I hope so. That's why I let you have the job. There was
a small road off to the left back about a mile. Does it show
on the map?" There was a new and rather businesslike
edge to Josh's words.

"There are a great many little roads on this map, Josh,"
Reva proclaimed a little worriedly.

"Anything called Gleaner's Corners? I saw a sign for
that a while ago. Said it was about ten miles."

Reva studied the paper in front of her, not wanting to
admit the mild apprehension she was experiencing. "I
. . . I can't find it, Josh. What," she paused, trying to sound
unconcerned, "what would you propose doing? Turning
back until we find a landmark we can identify?"

"I'm afraid we're not going much farther in either direction," he announced dryly.

"The chains . . ."

"Chains aren't going to do much good when I can't see
two feet in front of the car." With a decisive movement
Josh stopped the car and switched off the engine. Without
a word he removed the map from her lap and frowned
over it.

"What are you going to do?" Reva asked as he turned
and reached into the back seat for his new fleece-lined
jacket.

"I'm going to take a look around. See if I can find a road
sign or a cabin or something!" He shrugged into the suede-
and-fleece coat and pulled the collar up in preparation for
the driving snow. He looked every inch the northwestern
male, Reva thought abruptly. Josh was very good at
adapting. But she didn't say anything as he opened the car

201

door. "Stay inside, honey, and see if you can get a weather report on the radio."

"Yes, Josh," she agreed obediently, a wave of guilt washing over her at the thought that the mess was all her fault. She should have paid more attention to the map! "You . . . you won't be long?" She didn't want to tell him she was afraid he might get lost out there in the increasingly heavy snowstorm.

"I won't take any risks," he suddenly grinned, leaning briefly back into the car to drop a kiss on her slightly parted lips. "I have no intention of missing my own wedding night!" With that he was gone, leaving Reva to fiddle with the radio in an attempt to get some news.

As it turned out weather news was not hard to obtain. The storm had indeed arrived earlier than expected and it was turning out to be more violent than previously anticipated. It would last throughout the day and into the evening. Reva watched the snow pile rapidly on the road beside the car and bit her lip in vexation. Of all the stupid things to do! Josh would have every right to be more than mildly upset with her for having gotten them into this!

It was nearly half an hour before he returned and Reva, who hadn't dared to run the heater very much, was feeling quite chilled. She'd pulled her coat on over the expensive sweater and wool pants she was wearing and was wishing she'd bought the boots with warmth rather than style in mind when the opposite car door opened and Josh got in with a cold rush.

"Well," he allowed, slamming the door shut and running impatient fingers through his hair to remove the snow which had settled there, "I think I can safely say we're more than slightly off course."

"Oh, Josh, I'm sorry," Reva groaned, feeling a fool. "I wasn't paying proper attention and I . . ."

"We will," he interrupted firmly, "go into the subject of your map-reading abilities later. The important thing now is to get ourselves some shelter. Did you catch a weather report?" He settled into his corner of the car and eyed her interestedly. At least he didn't seem unduly upset as some men would have been in the circumstances, Reva thought gratefully. Quickly she told him the facts she'd heard on the news.

He nodded. "It certainly looks as if it's going to keep up for quite a while," he agreed, glancing out the window at the sheets of white descending from the sky. "Okay, I suppose we'd better get moving." He straightened and reached for the car keys.

"But where, Josh?" Reva demanded bewilderedly.

"I found an old cabin a few hundred feet back. It will take some doing hiking into it, but it can be done. Have you got all your warmest clothes on? I'll get the bags from the trunk."

Reva looked at him, common sense telling her that Josh might be very good in the jungles of South America but questioning his experience in mountain survival. Perhaps it would be safer to stay with the car. She'd heard tales of people wandering blindly in circles in a snowstorm until they'd frozen to death.

He glanced up and saw her watching him. "Worried, honey?" he asked with an unexpectedly understanding half smile. "Don't be. I'll take care of you."

Reva found herself smiling back, her uncertainties vanishing. Of course he would take care of her. She could trust him with her life. "I know," she whispered.

He watched her for a second longer and then nodded as if satisfied. Without another word he climbed out of the car and Reva stumbled behind him into the driving snow and cold. She shivered in reaction even though she had been expecting it. Josh pulled his worn leather bag and her own stylish one from the trunk, tucked them both under one arm, and then held out his hand to her.

Reva, thinking briefly of another occasion when she had taken his hand and followed him to safety, twined her gloved fingers in his and allowed him to lead her down the road.

They struggled through the snow, taking forever, it seemed to Reva, to reach the small, dark cabin a few hundred feet from the car. Josh was a rock of strength to which she clung during the difficult process.

"This is going to necessitate a small piece of breaking and entering," he told her when they eventually stood in front of the cabin door. "I hope you don't suffer from too many scruples."

"I'll look the other way," Reva managed with a pert smile as he went to work on the locked door. "Notice how I'm not asking where you learned such tricks?"

"Smart girl," he approved. "Refrain from that and I won't ask who taught you the fine art of map reading!"

"Are you going to bring that up again?" she complained as the door creaked and then swung inward. It was as cold inside the old cabin as it was outside. "I've already apologized!"

"Do I look like the vindictive sort?" he demanded in hurt astonishment as he pulled her inside, dropped the bags on the bare wooden floor, and shut the door.

"I have this awful premonition that on every anniversary in the years to come I'm going to be reminded of this little disaster!" Reva glanced around at the unprepossessing interior of the small wooden structure. It appeared to consist primarily of the living room which seemed to double as bedroom and kitchen. There was a tiny door off to the side which she hoped would lead to a few of the basic amenities.

"It will be a family tradition," Josh promised firmly, following her glance. "The water's probably been turned off to keep the pipes from freezing. I'll have a look around to see if I can turn it back on." He walked across to peer through a small window on the other side of the wall. "Good, there's firewood stacked on the back porch. We're going to be quite cozy and comfortable," he reported, sounding satisfied.

"Except for food," Reva said with a resigned sigh. "I was so looking forward to a hot toddy and a lovely big wedding-night dinner."

"Worried about your next meal already? Shades of South America!" Josh teased, striding over to a cupboard and opening it expectantly. Sure enough, a range of canned food stood arrayed on the shelf. "There you go," he grinned. "And so much easier than catching chickens!"

"I knew all I had to do was complain and you'd come through. Josh, the great provider!" Reva murmured, walking over to stand beside him. She put an arm around his waist and was immediately hauled close against his side.

"It comes from being an expert on marriage. A related field," he told her, dropping a husbandly kiss on the top of her head. "I suppose I'd better see about the water and a fire while there's still some light left. Your northwestern days sure are short!"

"Only during the winter," Reva laughed as he disengaged himself and started toward the door. "During the summer we'll have daylight until nine at night!"

"Promises, promises."

"You'll adapt," she smiled.

"Yes," he said, his hand on the door. "I will."

Reva turned interestedly toward the tiny kitchen as Josh disappeared. This was the night, she vowed to herself as she investigated the canned goods in detail. The night she would tell Josh about his real wedding present. She hummed gently as she dug out an old pan and discovered a can opener in the drawer.

"I must say," Reva murmured a long time later as she reclined beside her husband in front of a roaring fire, "you certainly do things in a first-class fashion. Leave it to Josh Corbett to turn up what is probably the only cabin within miles and have it well stocked into the bargain!" She saluted him with the paper cup of wine in her hand. "And that was a nice touch bringing along a bottle of my best wine."

Josh settled more deeply into the lumpy cushions of the old sofa and smiled blandly. "I had planned to open it in private tonight in our luxurious room at the lodge. A little something with which to toast my new bride." He lifted his own cup and met her eyes over the rim.

Reva met the honey-gold gaze and felt the now familiar tremor of response. She looked back at him, seeing the stirring of the male hunger there and that strange, almost hidden watchfulness which she hadn't been able to erase during the past three days.

"Do you know," he went on softly, breaking the small, curiously tense silence which had developed. "I'm seriously considering not beating you for that error in map reading this afternoon." There was a teasing quirk to his mouth and the crinkles around his eyes deepened.

"I'm so relieved," she smiled. "To what do I owe my deliverance?"

"To the fact that all this," he waved a hand vaguely around the cabin, "brings back memories of four months ago."

"I'd call it a definite step up," Reva observed, taking a

sip of wine. "At least you won't be sleeping with a gun within reach tonight!"

"No, thank God," he agreed with a genuine touch of fervor. "That's all behind me. All I want beside me in bed is you." He toasted her silently with the paper cup, watching the warmth climb into her cheeks as he swallowed the wine. "No more nightmares, Reva."

"No," she agreed softly, thinking that there had been none since the night she had asked him to marry her. It was as if something nervous and restless deep inside had been pacified at last. She had a feeling she would never again be troubled by the grim, recurring dream.

"Trust me?" he asked lightly. But there was something else in the question.

"I've always trusted you, Josh," she replied honestly.

"Except about the matter of me coming home to you when I'd finished in South America," he pointed out quietly. The firelight danced on the planes of his face and Reva couldn't quite read the expression there.

"Oh, I think I always knew you'd come after me," she admitted wryly. "Why do you imagine I changed apartments without leaving a forwarding address?"

"You did that deliberately," he agreed in an even tone. "Were you so afraid of taking another alley cat into your home?"

"No," Reva smiled and drew a deep breath. The time had come. "I was afraid of admitting that I loved that alley cat."

There was a stark silence as Josh stared at her. Was he really so surprised? she wondered dimly. Would he know what to do with her love?

"Reva," he whispered, setting his paper cup down on the old wooden table in front of the couch with unnatural care. His eyes never left hers and there was a sudden intense vulnerability and demand in them that made Reva want to do anything necessary to comfort him. Never had a man looked at her with so much longing, she realized.

"Reva, honey," he repeated a little thickly, not touching her although they sat so close. "Are you telling me that you do love me?"

"Yes," she whispered, blue-green eyes full of her emotions. "Why in the world do you think I married you?"

He licked his lower lip once before replying. She could feel the tension in him and wondered if perhaps she'd been precipitous in telling him. But this was her wedding night and what bride didn't want to be able to confess her love?

"Compassion, tenderness, gratitude," he replied slowly. "Any of the emotions I tried so hard to induce in you in order to get you to marry me."

Reva's small smile widened as she shook her head in exasperation. "I've got news for you, Josh Corbett, I would never marry a man for reasons like those!"

"You were so sure I was wrong for you," he said wonderingly, searching her face as if he still couldn't believe what she had said.

"Well, you'll have to admit, we do seem a bit mismatched," Reva said with gentle humor. "If it wasn't for your great adaptability, I'm not sure how we'd manage!"

"You and I," he told her with an abrupt fierceness, "can adapt to anything! Reva, why the hell haven't you told me?" He did touch her now, his large, competent hands reaching out to pull her tightly against him.

"I wasn't sure you wanted my love," she whispered, her head tilted back on his shoulder so that she could meet his eyes. "All you ever seemed to want was a home and a comfortable little woman."

"Comfortable little woman!" he repeated with a growl, his hands tightening. "That's about the last way I'd describe you! The only time you're comfortable is when you're lying in my arms, showing me how much you want me!"

"Thanks!" she muttered tartly.

"I knew I could make you want me, Reva," he went on, ignoring her comment. "But I thought it would be ages before you slipped over the edge and realized you could love me, too! And that's what I've wished for since the beginning, you little idiot. Why the hell do you think I married *you*?"

"You told me often enough," she pointed out politely. "You wanted a home."

"A home with you," he corrected feelingly. "Only with you." He rocked her gently against his strong, hard body and Reva nestled close, hope burning very brightly in her heart.

"Are you trying to tell me that you love me, too?" she asked him.

"From the first time I saw you. You were mine, Reva, from that moment when you took my hand and followed me out of that damned kitchen. I told you that before. You can't say you didn't know how I felt!" he husked deeply as he lifted a hand to stroke her cheek.

"Desire isn't . . . isn't the same as love, Josh." She tried to smile.

"You think I don't know that? At my age?" he chuckled. "My God, woman! I haven't exactly led a sheltered life up until now!"

Reva smiled with love. "But you will henceforth!" she promised.

"Sheltered by your love? Yes," he nodded with great certainty. "Just as you will be sheltered by mine. You won't hold my, er, checkered past against me?" He was

209

smiling but the tiniest hint of wariness had crept back into the lion gaze.

"Is it a very badly checkered past?" Reva asked teasingly.

"Would it matter?"

"No." She smiled up at him with complete honesty and was rewarded by a small kiss on the nose.

"Thank you, sweetheart," he whispered, and then his mouth quirked again. "I won't pretend to have been a saint, but there isn't any great, dark secret hanging over my head, either. I was always just a bit"—he hesitated— "restless, I guess you'd say. I kept looking for something and one thing led to another. Eventually I wound up working for the firm in Texas."

"Where all the female personnel are convinced you've either been an intelligence agent or a gunrunning pilot!" Reva murmured.

"Elaine told you that?" he grimaced.

Reva nodded.

"It's a wonder you didn't run out on me altogether at that point," he growled.

"Exactly what you'd deserve for trying to use another woman to manipulate me!" Reva told him mercilessly.

"It worked, didn't it?" he grinned back unrepentantly.

"I suppose it did hasten my decision," she groaned wryly. "I couldn't stand the thought of you going back to that awful job and that equally awful woman! Were you, Josh?" she added more soberly.

He didn't pretend to misunderstand. "I did a little flying for a time," he admitted quietly. "But it wasn't guns and it wasn't drugs. Mostly food and medical supplies. The only thing that made it a bit tricky was that some of the destinations were more isolated than others." He shrugged. "It provided me with a lot of contacts, though,

210

and they eventually became useful when I decided to seek more regular employment!"

"And the intelligence thing?" she pressed carefully, needing to know the whole truth.

He smiled offhandedly. "Sometimes I'd come back from the cargo-hauling trips with a few observations that were useful to certain people, but that was the extent of it."

"And there won't be any more of that?" Reva insisted tensely, a small frown narrowing her eyes as she watched him.

"Word of honor!" he vowed. And she believed him. She could trust Josh.

"Good," she breathed thankfully.

"Reva," he went on with an intent passion, "when I met you I found what I'd been looking for all those years. There was never any doubt in my mind from the first day that I had to have you. That I needed you. I love you, little one, and knowing that you love me makes me the most fortunate alley cat in the whole world!"

He kissed her with that huge, enveloping gentleness Reva responded to so instinctively and so quickly. This kiss was a soft thing to begin with, full of tenderness and restraint, as if he wanted desperately to convince her of his love. Reva stirred warmly as she sensed the tightly leashed need in him. Why hadn't she understood about his love before? Perhaps a woman always needed to hear it first in words. But having heard it, Reva knew she would always recognize it in his kiss. There was nothing else on earth quite like it for her.

"Josh, my darling, Josh," she breathed, circling his neck with her arms and holding his head close to hers. Her mouth opened like a flower beneath his lips and she felt the passion in him begin to slip the leash.

"Love me, Reva," he commanded, lifting his head for

a moment to seek out the expression in her love-softened eyes. "For the rest of our lives! I waited so very long for you, my darling."

"We've both waited a long time for love," she told him, her fingers threading through the silver at his temples. "But I don't regret it. I think it will mean more to us this way. I'll do everything in my power to make you happy and to make sure you don't regret giving up so much for me."

"I gave up nothing for you," he smiled, "but if you want to feel guilty about it and lavish a little extra attention on me, I won't complain."

"You and Xavier have far too much in common," she groaned feelingly. "Both out for all you can get!" That reminded her of something. "What would you have done if my best offer had been an affair instead of marriage?"

"Taken it," he sighed. "I'd have moved in and put my slippers under your bed. The only reason I didn't agree to it when you did offer was because I still had another ace up my sleeve to try!"

"Elaine?"

"Right. And luckily for me you came to your senses," he grinned with satisfaction.

"You are a cunning sort of husband," Reva noted with admiration. "I don't know why I let you manipulate me the way I do!"

"I like to think it's because love's made you conveniently blind to a few things."

"Just the opposite, I think," Reva said softly as a log crackled on the hearth. "It's made me see a few things I was never aware of before."

He lifted her hand and turned his lips against her palm in a soft, moving caress. Then he enclosed her smaller fingers in his and looked at her tenderly. "Do you suppose we owe all this to your having gotten us lost this afternoon?"

"No. I was going to tell you anyway tonight. It was going to be my wedding present to you, whether you wanted it or not!"

"I've wanted it, Reva," he assured her, pressing her slowly, heavily back against the worn cushions. "With everything that's in me, I've wanted it! But it was the one thing I was afraid to ask for!"

He stretched out on top of her, trapping her completely against the couch. She absorbed the beloved weight of him, thrusting her hands beneath his shirt until she could touch the warmth of his bare back.

The leaping flames of the fire flickered around them, bathing them in a heat that was as primitive as the passion which surged between them. Reva felt her clothes being removed slowly, lovingly, until she was warmed only by the fire and Josh's body.

"My sweet, loving, Reva," he murmured as he impatiently divested himself of his own garments. He wasn't satisfied until he had removed every barrier between them, but when he once again lowered himself along the length of her body Reva was aware of something different in his lovemaking.

And the difference made her smile with joy. The passion and the strength and the naked desire were still there, stronger than ever, but the wariness she had sensed in the past was gone.

"I love you, Josh, with every part of me," she managed breathlessly as his need overwhelmed them both.

"That's just as well," he declared with a kind of savage passion. "Because that's what I must have: every part of you!" He scorched her throat and shoulders with kisses no less fiery than the flames on the hearth.

"It works both ways," she told him thickly, her fingers clutched tightly in his dark hair as he bent his head to explore the small valley between her breasts.

"But you've had all of me from the beginning," he husked against her skin, his mouth now slightly below the curve of her bosom. "All you had to do was reach out and take it. I would never have given you less, little one."

His fingers touched one nipple, bringing it to life. Reva inhaled sharply and her hips moved instinctively.

"So loving and warm," he breathed, one hand reaching down to strain her against his hard thighs. "I lived with memories of your softness and your heat for four long months after I put you on that plane and I swore that when I found you again I would never let you go. The worst night I ever spent in my life was that first night back in your apartment, knowing you were so close at last!"

"And you thought everything was back to normal when I called out your name in my nightmare?" she teased huskily, her fingers dancing down his spine in a tiny, passionate exercise.

"Don't you dare laugh at me, witch," he growled, lifting his head to rake her face with lambent fire in the lion eyes. "You'll never know what restraint it required not to simply take you and have done with all the nonsense!"

"It wasn't nonsense!" she protested, vibrantly aware of his thumb stroking the sensitive inside of her wrist. She shivered in delight. "It was a self-defense mechanism. Besides, four months is a long time, Josh. We needed an opportunity to get used to each other again!"

"Excuses," he gritted, trailing his fingers from her wrist up to the inner part of her elbow and on to her shoulder. "But I can forgive all that now. I can forgive *anything* now. You're here in my arms at last with my ring on your finger and that's all that matters!"

"Love me, Josh!" Reva begged, feeling the magic and power in him set off one series of tremors after another.

"I will love you, little Reva," he vowed, responding to the urgency in her by pressing his weight more heavily against her softness. "I never had any choice," he added simply.

And then the words became less intelligible between them and the communication passed into that realm reserved for a man and a woman in love. Reva heard a voice cry out her husband's name at the violent and tender moment of union, felt him lay claim to her with a completeness which shocked her senses and which she knew instinctively she would never be able to escape.

But in that melding the claimer was as much the claimed. It could not be otherwise, for one cannot possess on such an intimate and far-reaching level unless one surrenders to the power of the possession. Reva sensed the depth of the mutual surrender and gloried in it. As it had been from the first, the act of love with Josh was an all-consuming thing, and tonight, with their love openly admitted, it bound completely. Neither would ever be free again.

Much later Reva opened her eyes as she felt Josh stir and slowly sit up beside her on the couch. She blinked sleepily up at him and smiled with all her love in her eyes.

"Where are you going?" she asked softly.

"To put another log on the fire. It's going to be cold tonight," he whispered, running a lazily possessive hand over her breasts and down to the swell of her hip. Her smile widened as she saw that he was reluctant to leave her long enough even to accomplish the small task. With a small groan he finally stood up, his strong, nude body reflecting the glow from the hearth.

Reva turned on her side, tucking a hand under one

cheek, and watched as he expertly banked the fire and fed it until it flamed brightly once again.

"We'll have to leave a note thanking the owner of this cabin," she remarked with a delicate yawn. He was so beautiful, she thought with pleasure.

"And some money to cover the cost of the food and wood," Josh agreed, coming back to stand beside her as she sprawled, totally relaxed, on the old sofa. "We'll tell them in the note that this was our wedding night. All the world loves a lover or something like that!"

"As long as you don't explain how we got here!" Reva grinned.

He laughed softly, richly. "Personally, I'm going to treasure the thought for years."

"You mean you're going to have a good laugh over it for years!" she accused.

"Well, you've got to admit, it is rather humorous that the great manager with the solid background in computers couldn't handle the little lines and dots on a road map!"

"I had an excuse," Reva told him tranquilly. "It was my wedding day. Brides are always nervous on their wedding days." She turned and stretched, tugging at the old army blanket they had discovered in a closet. Josh watched her pull it up to her chin and then he casually reached down and yanked it to a point below her feet. Reva pouted laughingly up at him.

"Tell me again how much you love me," he commanded, lowering himself once more to the couch beside her. He reached down and pulled the blanket up over both of them, cradling her close against him beneath it. He waited for her response, his chin in her hair. She could sense the catlike contentment in him.

"You're the greatest cure for nightmares I have ever

216

known," she murmured obediently. "Having you so close keeps all the nasties at bay."

"A man likes to feel needed," he retorted on a smothered laugh. "Sure you won't mind having me loafing about the place until I get another job?"

Reva started a bit. "Of course not," she said quickly, surprised. "I'm only hoping you won't get too bored or . . . or restless while you look for one."

"I intend to take my time. Who knows, I might like the career of a househusband!"

"You'll have to learn to fix something besides stew," Reva warned conversationally, yawning again.

"I've always done a pretty good job of seeing that you ate well, haven't I?" he mused complacently, sounding sleepy and happy. "Just think; no more secret dieting!"

"Don't remind me!" Reva groaned. "I shall probably put on twenty pounds the first month of our marriage. Every night will be an excuse to indulge!"

"I'll make sure you get enough exercise to keep you in reasonable trim," Josh promised.

There was a contented silence. And then Reva asked softly, "Are you quite sure you won't mind not having a job for a while?"

"Positive. I've earned a rest. No man has worked harder than I have during the past few days!" She could feel him smiling behind her ear. "And as I keep telling you, Reva Corbett, you married a man who's old enough to be sure of his own mind. I'm not particularly career oriented. I've always done whatever comes to hand. Fortunately, enough of what has come to hand has paid very well over the years. That dowry I mentioned has reached the point where it earns a fair amount on its own. Neither of us would starve if you lost your job tomorrow," he added dryly.

He sounded certain and Reva relaxed. Josh was adaptable. And he always knew what he wanted.

Like a cat, she told herself as her lashes closed in sleep, convinced she could almost hear him purring as she curled into his warmth. Like a battle-scarred and clever alley cat who has found a home at last. Which was precisely the case.

LOOK FOR NEXT MONTH'S
CANDLELIGHT ECSTASY ROMANCES™

25 FREEDOM TO LOVE, *Sabrina Myles*
26 BARGAIN WITH THE DEVIL, *Jayne Castle*
27 GOLDEN FIRE, SILVER ICE, *Marisa de Zavala*

Candlelight Ecstasy Romances

Love—the way you want it!

Candlelight Romances

From the author of *Evergreen*

RANDOM WINDS

by
BELVA PLAIN

From a quiet village in upstate New York to elegant house
parties in the English countryside...from the bedsides of the
rural poor to the frenetic emergency room of a Manhattan
hospital...from war-torn London to luxurious lovers' hide-
aways on the Riviera, here is the unforgettable story of three
generations of doctors—and of a love no human force could
surpress.

A Dell Book $3.50   (17158-X)

At your local bookstore or use this handy coupon for ordering:

Dell Bestsellers